LOVE AND OBSTACLES

RIVERHEAD BOOKS | A MEMBER OF PENGUIN GROUP (USA) INC. | NEW YORK | 2009

LOVE AND OBSTACLES

stories

ALEKSANDAR HEMON

RIVERHEAD BOOKS
Published by the Penguin Group
Penguin Group (USA) Inc., 375 Hudson Street, New York, New York 10014,
USA • Penguin Group (Canada), 90 Eglinton Avenue East, Suite 700, Toronto,
Ontario M4P 2Y3, Canada (a division of Pearson Canada Inc.) • Penguin Books Ltd,
80 Strand, London WC2R 0RL, England • Penguin Ireland, 25 St Stephen's Green,
Dublin 2, Ireland (a division of Penguin Books Ltd) • Penguin Group (Australia),
250 Camberwell Road, Camberwell, Victoria 3124, Australia (a division of Pearson
Australia Group Pty Ltd) • Penguin Books India Pvt Ltd, 11 Community Centre,
Panchsheel Park, New Delhi–110 017, India • Penguin Group (NZ), 67 Apollo Drive,
Rosedale, North Shore 0632, New Zealand (a division of Pearson New Zealand Ltd) •
Penguin Books (South Africa) (Pty) Ltd, 24 Sturdee Avenue, Rosebank,
Johannesburg 2196, South Africa

Penguin Books Ltd, Registered Offices: 80 Strand, London WC2R 0RL, England

The following stories first appeared, in different form, in *The New Yorker*:
"Stairway to Heaven," "Everything," "The Conductor," "Szmura's Room,"
"The Bees, Part 1," and "The Noble Truths of Suffering."

The lines from Arthur Rimbaud's "The Drunken Boat" and "Youth IV" are quoted
from Oliver Bernard's translations, in *Collected Poems* (Penguin Classics, 1987).

The lines from Zbigniew Herbert's "Report from the Besieged City" are quoted from
John Carpenter and Bogdana Carpenter's translation, in *Report from the Besieged City
and Other Poems* (Ecco Press, 1985).

Library of Congress Cataloging-in-Publication Data

Hemon, Aleksandar, date.
    Love and obstacles : stories / by Aleksandar Hemon.
       p.   cm.
    ISBN 978-1-59448-864-1
    I. Title.
    PS3608.E48L68   2009   2008050340
    813'.6—dc22

Printed in the United States of America
10 9 8 7 6 5 4 3 2 1

BOOK DESIGN BY STEPHANIE HUNTWORK

This is a work of fiction. Names, characters, places, and incidents either are the product
of the author's imagination or are used fictitiously, and any resemblance to actual
persons, living or dead, businesses, companies, events, or locales is entirely coincidental.

While the author has made every effort to provide accurate telephone numbers and
Internet addresses at the time of publication, neither the publisher nor the author
assumes any responsibility for errors, or for changes that occur after publication.
Further, the publisher does not have any control over and does not assume any
responsibility for author or third-party websites or their content.

For my parents

CONTENTS

LOVE AND OBSTACLES

Stairway to Heaven

t was a perfect African night, straight out of Conrad: the air was pasty and still with humidity; the night smelled of burnt flesh and fecundity; the darkness outside was spacious and uncarvable. I felt malarial, though it was probably just travel fatigue. I envisioned millions of millipedes gathering on the ceiling over my bed, not to mention a fleet of bats flapping ravenously in the trees under my window. The most troubling was the ceaseless roll of drums: the sonorous, ponderous thudding hovering around me. Whether it meant war, peace, or prayer, I could not tell.

I was sixteen, of the age when fear aroused inspiration, so I turned on the light, dug up a brand-new moleskin journal from my suitcase—the drums still summoning the vast forces of darkness—and wrote on the first page

Kinshasa 7.7.1983

only to hear my parents' bedroom door violently open, Tata cursing and stomping away. I leapt out of bed—Sestra, startled, started whimpering—and ran after Tata, who had already flipped on the lights in the living room. I bumped into Mama cradling her worrisome bosom in her arms. All the lights were on now; a gang of moths fluttered hopelessly inside a light fixture; there were cries and screams; cymbals crashed all around us. It was terrifying.

"Spinelli," Tata exclaimed against the noise. "What a dick."

Tata slept in flannel pajamas far more appropriate for an Alpine ski resort than for Africa—air-conditioning allegedly hurt his kidneys. But before he left the apartment, he also put on a pith helmet, lest his bald dome be exposed to draft. When he furiously vanished into the drumming murk of the stairway, Sestra, now crying, pressed her face against Mama's side; I stood in my underwear, my feet cold on the bare floor, a pen still in hand. The possibility of his not returning flickered in the darkness; it did not cross my mind to go after him; Mama did not try to stop him. The stairway light went on, and we heard a plangent chime. The drums were still rolling; another plaintive *ding-dong* fit snugly into the beat. Tata abandoned the bell and started pounding at the door, shouting in his stunted English:

"Spinelli, you are very crazy. Stop noise. We are sleep. It is four in the morning."

Our apartment was on the sixth floor; there must have been scores of people living in the building, but it appeared to have been abandoned in a hurry. The moment the stairway light went off again, the drumming stopped, the show was over. The door opened, and a nasal American voice said: "I'm sorry, man. I absolutely apologize."

By the time I went back to bed, it was dawning already. In the trees outside, a nation of birds replaced the blood-sucking bats and was now atwitter in a paroxysm of meaningless life. Sleeping and dreaming were beyond me now, nor could I write. Smoking on the balcony, I waited for everything to make sense until it couldn't. Down on the street a scarcely clad man squatted by a cardboard box with cigarettes lined up on it. There was nobody else on the street. It seemed that he was guarding the cigarettes from some invisible peril.

In the early eighties, Tata was absent, working in Zaire as a minor Yugoslav diplomat in charge of communications (whatever that meant). Meanwhile, in Sarajevo, I responded to the infelicity of adolescence and the looming iniquity of adulthood by retreating into books; Sestra was twelve, oblivious of the ache sprouting inside me; Mama was midlife miserable and lonely, which I could not see at the time, my nose stuck in a book. I read compulsively, only occasionally reaching the surface of common reality to take in a fetid breath of other people's existence. I would read all night, all day, instead of doing my homework; in school, I would read a book hidden under the desk, a felony frequently punished by a junta of class bullies. It was only in the imaginary space of literature that I felt comfortable and safe—no absent father, no depressed mother, no bullies making me lick the book pages until my tongue was black with ink.

I met Azra checking out books at the school library, and I immediately liked the readerly quietude on her bespectacled face. I walked her home, slowing down whenever I had something to say, stopping when she did. She had no inter-

3

est in *The Catcher in the Rye*; I had not read *Quo Vadis*, feigned interest in *The Peasant Uprising*. It was clear, however, that we shared a passion for imagining lives we could live through others—a necessary ingredient of any love. Quickly we found a few books we both liked: *The Time Machine*, *Great Expectations*, *And Then There Were None*. That first day we talked mostly about *The Dwarf from a Forgotten Country*. We loved it, even though it was a children's book, because we both could identify with a small creature lost in the big world.

We started dating, which meant that we often read to each other on a bench by the Miljacka, kissing only when we ran out of things to talk about, making out cautiously, as though letting it all go would have spent the quaint, manageable intimacy we had accrued. I was perfectly happy whispering a passage from *Franny and Zooey* or *The Long Goodbye* into her hair. So when Tata announced, upon his returning to Sarajevo on leave, that we would all spend the summer of '83 in Africa together, I felt a strange relief: if Azra and I were apart, we could resist the torturous temptation and eschew the taint that the body inescapably inflicts upon the soul. I promised I would write to her every day, in my journal, as letters from Africa would arrive long after my return. I would record every thought, I promised, every feeling, every experience, and as soon as I came back, we would reimagine it all together, reading, as it were, the same book.

There were many things I wanted to note down that first night in Kinshasa: the west ablaze, the east impenetrably dark as we crossed the equator at sunset; the perfect recollection of the smell of her hair; a line from *The Dwarf from a Forgotten Country* that we had both liked so well: *I have to find my way home before the fall, before the leaves cover the path.* But I wrote nothing and assuaged my conscience by ascribing it to the drumming disturbance. What I didn't write stayed in the back room of my mind, like the birthday presents I was not allowed to open until everyone had left the party.

In any case, the following morning Sestra was in the living room, looking with vague fascination at a puny man in a T-shirt depicting an angel shot in midair. Mama was sitting across the coffee table from him, listening intently to his high-pitched warbling, her legs crossed, the hem of her skirt curved over the northern hemisphere of her knee.

"*Svratio komšija Spinelli,*" she said. "*Nemam pojma šta priča.*"

"Good morning," I said.

"Good afternoon, buddy," Spinelli said. "The day is almost over." He exposed a set of teeth evenly descending in size from the center toward the cheeks, like organ pipes. Sestra smiled along with him; he had both of his hands parked on his thighs, and they were calmly immobile, resting before the next task. Which was to push apart the two curls parenthesizing his forehead. The curls instantly returned to the original position, their tips symmetrically touching his eyebrows.

That was the first time I faced Spinelli, and from that moment on, his face kept changing, although all the changes are unified now in the two wrinkles between his eyes, parallel like an equation sign, and that delicate, snarly smile that always came at the end of his sentences. He said: "Sorry for the noise. A bored dog does crazy things."

At sixteen I spent a lot of energy affecting boredom: the eyeroll; the terse, short answers to parental inquisition; the practiced blankness of expression in response to some real-life saga my parents were imparting. I had built an ironclad shield of indifference that allowed me to escape, read, and return to my cell without anyone's noticing. But the first week in Africa, the boredom was real. I could not read; I kept scanning the same—twenty-seventh—page of *Heart of Darkness* and could not move beyond it. I tried to write to Azra, but found nothing to say, probably because there was so much to say.

There was certainly nothing to do. I was not allowed to go out alone into the human jungle of Kinshasa. For a while I watched TV, broadcasting Mobutu's rants and commercials featuring cans of coconut oil floating in the blue sky of affordable happiness. Once or twice, in the middle of the day, I even felt a rare, inexplicable desire to be with my family, but Tata was at work; Sestra guarded her budding sovereignty with her Walkman turned way up; Mama was remote, interned in the kitchen, probably crying. The ceiling fan spun sluggishly, incessantly, cruelly reminding me that time here passed at the same mind-numbingly slow speed.

Tata was a great promiser, a fabulist of possibilities. Back in Sarajevo, he had projected on the vast, blank canvas of our socialist provincialism the Kinshasa that was a hive of neocolonial pleasures: exclusive clubs with pools and tennis courts; diplomatic receptions frequented by the international jet set and spies; cosmopolitan casinos and exotic lounges; safaris in the wilderness and Philippe, a native cook whom he had hired away from a Belgian by increasing his wage to a less piddling amount. That first, uneventful week these promises were drably betrayed—not even Philippe showed up for work. When Tata came home from the embassy, we had humdrum dinners Mama improvised from what she had discovered in the fridge: wizened peppers and sunken papayas, peanut paste and animal flesh that may have been goat meat.

Determined to dispel the cloud of tedium hanging over us, Tata finally put a call in to the Yugoslav ambassador and invited ourselves to his residence in Gombe, where all the important diplomats lived. The mansions there were large, the lawns were wide, majestic flowers bloomed in impeccably groomed bushes, the venerable Congo flowed serenely. His Excellency and his excellent wife were polite and devoid of any human vigor or storytelling talent. We sat in their receiving room, the adults passing around statements ("Kinshasa is strange"; "Kinshasa is really small") like a sugar bowl. Exotic trophies were carefully positioned around the room: a piece of Antwerp bobbin lace on the wall; an ancient Mesopotamian rock on the coffee table; on the bookshelf, a picture of Their Excellencies on a snow-capped mountain. A servant with an implausible red sash brought in the drinks—Sestra and I were each given a glass of lemonade with a long silver spoon. I dared not move, and when Sestra, abruptly and inexplicably, rolled like a happy dog on the ankle-deep Afghan carpet, I feared our parents would renounce us.

As soon as we returned home, I went up to Spinelli's place. He opened the door wearing the shot-angel shirt and shorts, his legs stilt-thin. He did not seem at all surprised to see me, nor did he ask what brought me around. "Come on in," he said, smoking, a drink in his hand, music blasting behind him. I lit up; I had not smoked all day, and I was starved for nicotine. The smoke descended into my lungs like feathery silk, then out, thickly, through the nose; it was so beautiful I was breathless and dizzy. Spinelli was playing air drums along with the loud music, a half-burnt cigarette in the center of his mouth. "'Black Dog,'" he said. "God damn." In the far corner, right under the window, was a set of drums; the golden cymbals trembled under the stream from the air conditioner.

Playing imaginary drum solos and bridges, Spinelli made unsolicited confessions: He had grown up in a rough Chicago neighborhood and beat it as soon as he could; he had lived in Africa forever; he worked for the U.S. government, and could not tell me what his job was, for if he did he would have to kill me. He started each sentence sitting down, then finished standing up; the next one was accompanied by banging of the invisible drums. He never stopped moving; the space organized itself around him; he exuded so much of himself I felt absent. Only after I had, exhausted, left his place could I really think at all. And so I thought that he was a true American, a liar and a braggart, and that hanging out with him was far more stimulating than the shackles of family life or the excellent diplomats in Gombe. At some point during his streaming, restless monologue, he christened me, for no apparent reason, Blunderpuss.

I went back upstairs a couple of days later, and then again the following day. Mama and Tata seemed fine with that, for if I took my boredom away, we could all avoid long stretches of crabby silence. They must have thought also that engaging with the real world and its inhabitants without actually going out was good for me, and I got to practice my English too. As for me, I smoked at Spinelli's as much as I wanted; the music was much louder than my parents would ever permit; he poured whiskey in my glass before it was half empty. He even showed me how to play drums a bit—I loved smashing the cymbals. But most of all I enjoyed his narratives: he delivered them slouching back in the sofa, blowing cigarette smoke toward the fast-spinning ceiling fan, sipping his J&B, interrupting his delivery for a solo in a Led Zeppelin song. There might be a taint of death, a flavor of mortality, in lies, but Spinelli's were fun to listen to.

He had run a cigarette-selling business in high school, and had regularly had sex with his geography teacher. He had hitchhiked across America: in Oklahoma, he drank with Indians who fed him mushrooms that took him to where their spirits lived—the spirits had big asses with two holes, which smelled equally of shit; in Idaho, he lived in a cave with a guy who watched the sky all day long, waiting for a fleet of black helicopters to descend upon them; he smuggled cattle from Mexico into Texas, cars from Texas to Mexico. Then he was in the Army: avoiding rough deployment by applying onion to his dick so as to fake an infection; whoring around in Germany, cutting up a Montenegrin pimp in a disco. Then Africa: sneaking into Angola to help out Savimbi's freedom fighters; training the Ugandan special forces with the Israelis; setting up a honey trap in Durban. He told his tales laterally, moving across his life without regard for chronology.

Afterward, I would lie in my bed, trying to organize his stream of consciousness in my giddy head so that I could write it down for Azra. But I failed, for now I could see the loopholes in the texture of his tales, the inconsistencies and contradictions and the plain bullshit. The stories were unimpeachable when he was telling them, but would have been obvious lies if written down. Once I was out of his proximity, he made little sense; he had to be physically present in his own narratives to make them plausible. Therefore I sought his presence; I kept going upstairs.

One night I went up, but Spinelli was all dressed and ready to go, wearing an unbuttoned black shirt, reeking of shower and cologne, a gold chain dangling below his Adam's apple. He lit a cigarette at the doorstep, inhaled, and said, "Let's go!" and I followed without a question. It did not even cross my mind to let my parents know where I was going. They never came to check on me when I was upstairs, and the boredom I had endured certainly entitled me to some adventure. It turned out we were going to a casino around the corner.

"The guy who owns the casino is Croatian," Spinelli said. "Used to be in the Foreign Legion, fought in Katanga, then in Biafra. I don't wanna know the things he did. We do business sometimes, and his daughter likes me pretty well too."

I could not see his lips moving as we walked, his voice was disembodied. I was vibrating with curiosity, but could not think of anything to ask him: the reality he implied was so solid as to be impassable. We turned the corner, and there was a splendid neon sign reading PLAYBOY CASINO, the S and O flickering uncertainly. A few white cars and military jeeps were parked on the gravel lot. On the stairs stood a few hookers in ridiculously high heels, neither climbing nor descending, as though afraid they might fall if they moved. But move they did as we passed them; one of them grabbed my forearm—I felt her long nails bending against my sweaty skin—and turned me toward her. She wore a helmetlike purple wig and earrings as elaborate as Christmas ornaments, her breasts pushed up by her tiny bra so I could see half of her left nipple. I stood petrified until Spinelli released me from her grip. "You don't fuck much, Blunderpuss, do you?" he said.

Three men were sitting at the roulette table, all plain drunk, their heads falling on their chests between the revolutions of the wheel. The heavy fog of masculine recklessness hung over the table, the green of the felt fractured by the piles of colorful chips. One of the men won, snapped out of his torpor to take the chips with both of his arms, as if embracing a child. "Watch the croupier steal from them," Spinelli said with delight. "They're going to lose it all before they get another drink, then they'll lose some more." I did watch the croupier, but could not see how the stealing happened: when they won, he pushed the chips toward them; when they lost, he raked the pile toward himself. It all seemed simple and honest, but I believed Spinelli, fascinated with abomination. I started composing a description of this place for Azra. The hallway of hell: the cone of smoke rising to the light above the blackjack table; the hysterical flashing of the two slot machines in the corner; the man standing at the bar in the attire of a plantation owner, light linen suit and straw hat, his right hand hanging down from the bar like a sleeping dog's head, a ribbon of cigarette smoke slowly passing his knuckles.

"Let me introduce you to Jacques," Spinelli said. "He's the boss."

Jacques put the cigarette in his mouth, shook Spinelli's hand, then looked me over without saying a word.

"This is Blunderpuss, he's Bogdan's kid," Spinelli said. Jacques's face was perfectly square, the nose perfectly triangular; his neck was less like a tree stump than a stovepipe of flesh. He bespoke the chummy ruthlessness of someone whose life was organized around his profit and survival; as far as he was concerned, I did not exist in the world of straightforward facts. He put out his cigarette and, in English marred with clunky Croatian consonants, said to

Spinelli: "What I am going to do with those bananas? They are rotting."

Spinelli looked at me, shook his head in bemused disbelief, and said: "Put them in a fruit salad."

Jacques grinned back at him and said: "Let me tell you joke. Mother has very ugly child, horrible, she goes on train, sits in *coupe*. People come in her *coupe*, they see child, is very ugly, they cannot look, they leave, go away, disgusting child. Nobody sits with them. Then comes man, smiles at mother, smiles at child, sits down, reads newspapers. Mother thinks, Good man, likes my child, is real good man. Then man takes one banana and asks mother: 'Does your monkey want banana?'"

Spinelli didn't laugh, not even when Jacques repeated the punch line: "Does your monkey want banana?" Instead, he asked Jacques: "Is Natalie here?"

I followed Spinelli through a bead curtain into a room with a blackjack table and four men sitting at it; they all wore uniforms, one of them sand-khaki, the other three olive-green. Natalie was the dealer, her fingers long and limber as she dealt the cards; her pallor was luminous in the dark room; her arms were skinny, no muscles whatsoever; she had bruises on her forearms, scratches on her biceps. On her shoulder she had a vaccine mark, like a small-coin imprint. Spinelli sat at the table and nodded at her, slamming a cigarette pack against his palm. Her cheeks rose, quotation marks forming around her smile. Having dealt the cards, she raised her hand, gently, as though lifting a veil, and scratched her forehead with her pinkie; her hair, pulled tightly into a ponytail, shimmered on her temples. She blinked slowly, calmly; it appeared that pulling her long eyelashes apart required effort. I stood in the dark enthralled, smoking, my heart beating fast, but calmly. Natalie was from out of this world, a displaced angel.

From thereon in, for a while, there were the three of us. We went places: Spinelli driving his Land Rover reeking of dogs and rope, drumming on the wheel, slapping the dashboard instead of a cymbal, calling Natalie his Monkeypie; Natalie smoking in the passenger seat, looking out; me in the back, the breeze from the open window blowing the cigarette smoke intoxicatingly mixed with her smell directly in my face. The three of us: Spinelli, Monkeypie, Blunderpuss, like characters in an adventure novel.

On July 27—I remember because I made another attempt at writing—we went to the Cité to look for Philippe, who still hadn't shown up for work. Presumably, this was a means for Spinelli to expiate his drumming sins, arranged between Tata and him. Spinelli and Natalie picked me up at the crack of dawn; the light was still diffused by the residues of the humid night. We drove toward the slums, against the crowd marching in antlike columns: men in torn shorts and shreds for shirts; women wrapped in cloth, carrying baskets on their heads, swollen-bellied children trotting by their sides; emaciated, long-tongued dogs following them at a hopeful distance. I had never seen anything so unreal in my life. We turned onto a dirt road, which turned into a car-wide path of mounds and gullies. The Land Rover stirred up a galaxy of dust, even when moving at a low speed. Shacks misassembled from rusty tin and cardboard were lined up above a ditch, just about to tumble in. I understood what Conrad meant by *inhabited devastation*. A woman with a child tied to her back dipped clothes into tea-colored water and slapped the wet tangle with a tennis racket.

Soon a shouting mob of kids was running after the car. "Check this out," Spinelli said, and hit the brakes. The kids slammed into the Land Rover; one of them fell on his ass, others backed off and watched, scared, the Land Rover moving on forward. "Oh, stop it!" Natalie said. As soon as the car caught some speed, the kids were running after it again; they didn't see a Land Rover in the Cité too often. Spinelli hit the brakes again, slapping his thigh with glee. I could see the face of the tallest boy smash against the back window, blood blurting out of his nose. Spinelli's laughter was deep-chested, like the bark of a big dog, ending with a sucking noise. It was infectious; I was roaring with laughter myself.

We stopped in front of a church, where a choir was singing: thorough, somber voices. Spinelli went in to leave a message for Philippe; Natalie and I stayed behind. He pushed his way through the kids, who parted, murmuring: "*Mundele, mundele.*" I wanted to say something that would delight Natalie, but all I could think of was to ask: "What are they saying?" "It means 'skinless,'" she said. The tall boy was still bleeding, but could not take his eyes off Natalie.

She took a picture of him; he wiped his bloody nose and turned away from the camera; a few other kids covered their faces with their hands. I didn't know what to say, so I closed my eyes and pretended to nap.

"You gonna have to get yourself a new cook, Blunderpuss," Spinelli said, climbing into his seat. "That's Philippe's funeral they're singing for. The man's happily dead."

From the Cité we went to the market—Le Grand Marché—and wandered around; it was too early to go home. All the smells and colors, all the stuff of the world: snakes, bugs, rats and rodents, clucking chickens and plucked fowl, flat fish, long fish, square fish, and skinned mongrel creatures that seemed to have been slapped together in hell. Spinelli bartered in Lingala and English, plus hands and grimaces. He pretended to be interested in a dried monkey, whose hands grasped nothingness with unappetizing despair; he picked through yams but didn't buy any. Natalie took pictures of terrified goats waiting to be slaughtered under the counter, of eels still fidgeting in a beaten pot, of worms squirming in a shoe box, which the woman who was selling them protected from the lens with a newspaper.

These people had no abstract concept of evil, Spinelli said, like we did; for them it was black magic coming from a particular person, so if you wanted to get rid of the evil spell you eliminated the guy. The same thing with the good: it was not something you could aspire to, like we did; you couldn't get it, either you had it or you didn't. He delivered his anthropological lecture while bargaining over an enormous, baroque cluster of bananas; he bought it for nothing and loaded it on his shoulder. You could not die of hunger here, he said, 'cause bananas and papayas grew like weeds everywhere. That was why these people never learned to work; they never had to harvest and store food to survive. And their blood was thicker too, which explained why they slept all the time.

Nobody slept in the Grand Market; everybody was yelling, heckling, bargaining. A mass of people followed us, offering things we could not possibly need: toilet brushes, knitting needles, figurines carved out of what Spinelli claimed was human bone. I ventured to buy a bracelet made of elephant hair and ivory, but only after he had inspected it. It was supposed to be a gift for Azra.

Later that same day, we went to the InterContinental. We trod the leopard-patterned carpet to the lounge, where a ponytailed pianist played "As Time Goes By." We got colorful cocktails with tiny umbrellas stuck in unknown fruit. There were men in Zairian attire: wide collars, no ties, bare chests with a lot of gold, hands bejeweled. Spinelli called them the Big Vegetables; they liked to stick out of Mobutu's ass. And those expensive white whores with them came from Brussels or Paris; they spread their legs for two or three months, then took a little pouch of diamonds back home to live it up for the rest of the year. And that man over there was Dr. Slonsky, a Russian who had come twenty years earlier, when you had to import ass-wipes from Belgium. He used to be Mobutu's personal physician, but currently he did only the Big Vegetables—Mobutu had a Harvard graduate taking care of him. Slonsky was constantly depressed, because he liked to shoot up.

Natalie sucked at her straw, not listening, as if she had heard it all already. "Are you okay, Monkeypie?" Spinelli asked her. I wanted to show, in solidarity with her, that I could not be fooled by Spinelli's gossip, but in truth I was mesmerized.

Then there was Towser the Brit. His was a garden of earthly delights, with flowers you could not begin to name; his wife worked at the British embassy. And that scruffy youngster sitting next to him was their Italian boyfriend. They were talking to Millie and Morton Fester. They were New Yorkers, but liked to spend time in Africa; they dealt in tribal art, that kind of crap, most of it pilfered away from the natives by the Big Vegetables. Millie wrote fancy porn novels; Morton used to be a photographer for *National Geographic*, trawled the dark continent for images of bizarre animals. He had a full head of hoary hair, and huge glasses that extended beyond his sunken cheeks; she had the yellow teeth of a veteran smoker. Spinelli actually waved at them, and Morton waved back. Somehow, the waving confirmed Spinelli's stories; he conjured them into existence with the motion of his hand.

Then we were joined by Fareed, a Lebanese whose head was smooth like a billiard ball and whom Spinelli affectionately called Dicknose. He bought us a round of drinks, and before I could even agree to it, we went up to Dicknose's room, where he opened a black briefcase for us. There was a velvet cloth in it; he unwrapped it and proudly exhibited a tiny heap of uncut diamonds, sparkling like teeth in a toothpaste commercial. The diamonds had just arrived from Kasai, Dicknose said, fresh from the bowels of the earth. Natalie touched the heap with the tips of her fingers, worried that those nuggets of light might vanish; her nails were bitten to a bloody pulp. "All you need to make your girlfriend here happy, Blunderpuss, is twenty-five thousand dollars," Spinelli said. Natalie looked at me and smiled, confirming the price.

From the InterContinental, we drove to Spinelli's place through the haze of my exhilaration and the local humidity, past the American embassy, an eight-story building surrounded by a tall wall. Bored guards smoked behind the iron-grille gate. On the top of the embassy was a nest of sky-begging antennas. I imagined a life of espionage and danger; I imagined letters I would send to Azra from behind enemy lines; they would be signed with a false name, but she would recognize my handwriting: *When you get this letter, my dear, I will be far beyond the reach of your love.*

"This is where I defend freedom so I can pursue happiness," Spinelli said. "One day I'll take you there, Blunderpuss."

As we climbed the stairs of our building, I walked by the apartment where my family should have been having dinner, but it felt as though they were not there, as though our place were empty. It could have been frightening, the absence, but I was too excited to care.

Straight from the doorstep, Spinelli went to his magnetophone and turned it on. The reels started revolving slowly, indifferently. "Ladies and gentlemen, 'Immigrant Song,'" he hollered, and then howled along with the music:

"AaaaAaaaAaaaaaaAaaa Aaaa . . ."

I put my hands on my ears to exaggerate my suffering, and Natalie laughed. Still screaming, Spinelli rummaged through the debris on his coffee table until he found what I instantly identified as a joint. He interrupted his howl to light it up, suck it in briskly, and pass it on to Natalie. I was innocent in the way of drugs, but when Natalie, holding her breath so that her eyes were bulging and, somehow, bluer for that, when Natalie offered it to me, I took it and inhaled as much as I could. Naturally, I coughed it all out immediately, saliva and phlegm erupting toward her and Spinelli. Her laughter was snorty, pushing her cheek apples up, dilating her nostrils—she had to lie down and hold her tummy. A chenille of snot hung from my nose, nearly reaching my chin. "If you can't stand the heat, Blunderpuss," Spinelli whinnied, "stay out of the oven." Well, I was enjoying the oven, and once the cough subsided, I sipped the smoke out of the joint and kept it in my lungs, resisting the devilish scratching in my throat, waiting for the high to arrive.

Spinelli sat at his drum set and grabbed the sticks. He listened intently to a different song now, waiting, only to hit the timpani hard, playing along with the music, biting his lips to express passion.

"The greatest goddamn bridge in the history of rock 'n' roll," he said. He attacked the timpani again, even though the song moved on, and he kept doing it. I recognized the beat: it was what had frightened us the first night.

"What's the name of that song?" I asked.

"'Stairway to Heaven,'" Spinelli said.

"It sounds so African."

"That ain't African. That's Bonzo, white as they come."

Natalie took the joint from my hand; her fingers were soft and cold, her touch eerily gentle. I leaned back and stared at the fan revolving frenziedly, as if a helicopter were buried upside down in the ceiling. Spinelli stopped drumming to get a hissy puff.

"See," he said, exhaling, "you're just an innocent kid, Blunderpuss. When I was your age I did things I wouldn't do now, but I did them then so I don't have to do them now."

He was rewinding the tape, pressing the Stop and Play buttons alternately, trying to find the beginning. The tape squealed and yelped until he pinpointed the moment of silence before "Stairway to Heaven."

"There's so much you don't know, son. Do you know what you don't know?"

"No, I don't."

"You have no idea how much you don't know. Before you know anything, you have to know what you don't know."

"I know."

"The fuck you do."

"Leave him alone," Natalie said, dreamily.

"Shut up, Monkeypie." He took another puff, spat on

the minuscule butt, and flicked it toward the ashtray on the coffee table, missing by a yard. Then he asked me:

"Why are you here?"

"Here? In Kinshasa?"

"Forget Kinshasa, Blunderpuss. Why are you here on this goddamn planet? Do you know?"

"No," I had to admit. "I don't."

Natalie sighed, suggesting she knew where it was all heading.

"Exactly," Spinelli said, and smashed a cymbal with the sticks. "That's exactly your problem."

"Are you okay, sweetheart?" Natalie asked me, extending her hand to touch me, but she couldn't reach me and I couldn't move.

"Yeah, sure," I said.

"Listen to him: 'Yeah, sure,'" Spinelli said. "He sounds like an American."

"Let him be."

But "Stairway to Heaven" was picking up, the drums kicking in. "That's the way." Spinelli leapt in excitement. "There is always a tunnel at the end of the light."

By this time he was leaning over me, blocking the view of the ceiling fan.

"Steve," Natalie said without conviction. "Leave him alone."

"He is alone," Spinelli said. "We live as we dream. Fucking alone."

"That's Conrad," I said.

"What's that?"

"That's Joseph Conrad."

"No, no, no, no, never, sir. That ain't no Joe Conrad. That's the truth."

He played the "Stairway to Heaven" bridge over my head, closing his eyes, curling his lower lip. Natalie leaned away from me, slipped her hand between her cheek and a pillow and closed her eyes, producing a celestial smile. He dropped next to me, his back to Natalie's stomach.

"There's a tribe here," he went on, his voice lowered, "that believes that the first man and woman slid down from the skies on a rope. God let them down on a rope, they untied themselves and the boss pulled the rope up. And that's exactly what happened, my friend. We were dropped down here and we wanna go back up, but there's no rope. So here you are, Blunderpuss, and the rope is gone."

He spread his arms to point at our surroundings: the coffee table with a pile of formerly glossy *National Geographics*, on top of which was Natalie's camera; an overflowing ashtray and a bottle of J&B; ebony sculptures of stolid elephants and twiggy warriors, one of them draped in his T-shirt.

"But we can at least try to get up as high as possible," he said, and excavated a tinfoil nugget from his pocket, unwrapped it with delectation, and showed me a lump of olive-green paste at its heart. "That's why God gave us Afghanistan."

The day I smoked pot for the first time was also the day I smoked hashish for the first time. Spinelli chipped slivers off the lump, then stuffed it down the narrow asshole of a clay pipe, murmuring: "Yessiree, Bob!" to himself. This time

I had no trouble inhaling and releasing the smoke impressively slowly.

"I'm here," Natalie said, and I passed the pipe to her. She smoked on her back, her eyes still closed. The smoke crawled out of her mouth, as though she were not breathing at all.

"See, I was much like you when I was a kid. I looked for hours at the map of South America, and Africa, and Australia. I thought: There the fuck I go," Spinelli said.

He stared at me for an endless moment, as though he were looking at the map again. His eyes were dim; I had a hard time keeping my eyes open.

"And here I am. Because I believe in something. Everybody's gotta believe in something. You gotta know your way."

He leaned back into Natalie, who sneezed like a cat but remained impassive. My head and stomach were completely empty. I tried to inhale some air to fill the vacuum inside me, but it didn't work. I was gasping, rapidly deflating, and it sounded like a giggle—I heard myself as someone else.

"You might wanna munch on a banana or something," he said. "You are pale as shit." Abruptly he stood up, startling me, and charged off to the kitchen. Natalie's face was ashen, her lips pink; a single hair stretched from her forehead to her mouth, where it curved toward the right corner. Before I could make any decision, I inhaled and leaned toward her, planting a kiss where the hair touched her mouth. She opened her eyes and widened her smile until I could see her tongue tip protruding between her teeth.

I retreated into my throne of stupor just as Spinelli came

back with a huge, blazingly yellow banana in hand. He offered it to me and said:

"Would the monkey like a banana?"

The monkey ate the banana, promptly passed out, and dreamt of two women, one fat, one slim, knitting black wool to the rhythm of drums, chanting angrily: "Spinelli! Spinelli! Spinelli!" Whereupon I woke to see Tata in his pith helmet and flannel pajamas yelling at Spinelli and shaking an enraged, ruddy finger before his face. Spinelli had his hands on his hips, and they slowly curled into fists; he was about to punch my father. I wanted to charge to Tata's defense, but my limbs would not move. Natalie sat up and said: "Steve, let it go, let Bogdan take the boy home." The bunched-up hair on the right side of her head had the shape of a harp, or half a heart.

"All right, man, I apologize. We were just partying a little," Spinelli said. "Hopefully, it's all bridge under the water."

Walking downstairs was much like crossing an underwater bridge: an invisible stream pushed against my knees, I could not feel the solid concrete under my feet. Tata practically carried me, his hand grasped my flesh ungently, sternly. He talked to me, but I could hear only the tone of his voice: it was angry and quivering. Downstairs, Mama and Sestra sat on the couch like a two-member jury; Sestra watched me with slumberous amusement; Mama's face was awash in tears. For some reason, it was all funny to me, and when Tata dropped me into the armchair across from them, I slid down to the floor and convulsed in laughter.

Later, in the middle of the night, I tottered to the kitchen, found the trash bin in the darkness, pressed the pedal to open the lid, and then pissed a thick, pleasurable stream into its mouth.

There was no talk given by my parents, no warnings about drugs and alcohol, no lectures about self-respect, no complaints about cleaning up the piss lake on the kitchen floor. They just stared at me, mute, across the dinner table: Tata worrisomely pouted, contemplating the troubling questions of my future; Mama pressed her hand against her cheek, shaking her head at the extraordinary bad luck in having me for a son, tear gems forming in the corners of her eyes.

I was forced to go everywhere they went: to Lolo La Crevette, where we devoured shrimp with Vaske, a malarial Macedonian prone to delivering unhurried reports on his talkative cockatoo; to the Portuguese club, where I watched two decrepit Frenchmen ineptly play tennis and scream at a skinny boy fetching their scattershot balls; to the Belgian supermarket, pristinely overlit, where everyone was immaculately white, as if the place had been magically transported from the pallid heart of Brussels. I often carried *Heart of Darkness* around and tried to read when no one was talking to me, which was very far from often enough. All I wanted was to be alone.

But I was alone only when I smoked on the balcony in the tarrish heat, hoping to see Spinelli or Natalie on the street, and I never did. There was no shuffling of the feet upstairs, no slamming of the door, no drumming or hollering along with Led Zeppelin. When I thought of our time together, I could not recall our doing anything or being anywhere. All I could recollect was his voice, mouthy and squeally, reciting his adventures: Spinelli going up the Congo with a crew of mercenaries, looking for a fallen Soviet satellite; Spinelli running into cannibals who thought he was a god because he produced a coin from behind the ear of a warrior; Spinelli in Angola, submerged in a shallow river up to his eyes, like a hippo, invisible to the Cuban patrol searching for him; Spinelli with a defector-to-be in a Durban restaurant, spooning raw monkey brain out of a cut-open skull.

One Sunday we went to the Czechoslovakian ambassador's garden party in Gombe. There was beer and champagne, *maracujá* juice and punch; there were piles of nibblets and fruit, offered on vast trays by a couple of humble servants; there were the blonde twin daughters of the Romanian ambassador; there were Our Excellency and his wife; and there were a lot of wily communist kids scurrying around and taunting the angry chimpanzee in a cage by the garden shed. I wanted to find a quiet spot and read, but Tata compelled me to join a volleyball game. We played on the sandlot between two enormous palms whose leaves, like monster quills, hung high over the net. We were on the same team with a squat Bulgarian whose many gold chains rattled every time he swung to miss the ball, and with the

Romanian twins, who leapt for the ball gracefully and fell down on their asses stupidly. Fortunately, there was also a Russian named Anton, tall and lanky, potato-nosed, gray-eyed. He was by far our best player and handily destroyed the other team. He showed me how to make my fingers flexible so the ball floated high enough for Tata to smack it into our ambassador's excellently flabby flesh.

Anton was the only man who did not smoke or drink after the game; indeed, he did not even drink water; he knew how to retain control. I followed him and Tata to a table under an enormous umbrella; they spoke Russian to each other, and Anton's voice was deep and curt, used to giving orders. He tapped on the table with his agitated finger; Tata threw his arms up; they looked at me every now and then. I did not understand what they were talking about, but I could hear the name Spinelli rising out of the Slavic gibberish. A flare of hope went up in my chest, and when I turned around I saw Natalie walking barefoot toward me in a diaphanous white dress, the sun transforming her tresses into a halo. But it was in fact one of the Romanian twins, guzzling beer out of a large mug, two streaks curving from the corners of her mouth toward her bepimpled chin.

Soon thereafter we went east for the promised safari. A man was waiting for us on the tarmac of the Goma airport; we saw him as soon as we stepped out of the plane. He wore dark shades, a white shirt, and a black tie; he walked up to

Tata and shook his hand diplomatically, as though welcoming a dignitary. He spoke to him in French, then switched to English for us—or me, rather, even if he was looking at Mama—welcoming us to Goma and wishing us a pleasant stay at the Karibu Hotel, as well as a successful safari. His name was Carlier; he assured us he was at our service, and kissed Mama's hand while she tried to extract it from his grip. He stroked Sestra's hair and nodded at me, as if he thought I was tough and he respected it.

Carlier was slurring his words, and I could not figure out whether that was his accent or he was drunk. Except for his shades and a large diamond ring on his middle finger, he resembled a butcher in a poor neighborhood: a heavy, fat-rounded head, large ears with meaty earlobes, blood speckles on his mercilessly scraped face. He bribed our way through the ovenlike airport, extending his money-stuffed hand to uniformed officers and importantly frowning Small Vegetables. Outside the airport, he chased away a swarm of cabbies and crap-hawkers and led us to a van next to which a man stood at attention in a full suit with a tightly knotted tie. Carlier barked at him and he leapt like a leopard to open the door for us.

The streets of Goma were enveloped in roiling clouds of black dust. In an uncanny, disturbing moment, I recognized that everyone in sight was barefoot, and I could not remember what the purpose of shoes was. But then I saw booted policemen standing on the porches, leaning against the walls, like idle villains in westerns, and the world of straightforward facts was restored. When we stopped to let a skittish herd of goats pass, nobody approached the van to offer us carved human bones or knitting needles.

"You make a right turn here," Carlier said, "and you are in Rwanda."

We turned left, got out of town, and drove through the fields of black lava rock surrounding intermittent islands of jungle verdure. A gray mountain beyond the green-and-black landscape exuded smoke; the earth appeared unearthly. "Nyiragongo," Carlier said, as if the word were self-explanatory.

The Karibu Hotel consisted of huts scattered along the shore of Lake Kivu, which, Carlier told us gleefully, contained no life: the last time Nyiragongo had erupted, the volcanic gases killed every living creature in it. Sestra and I shared one of the huts, redolent of clean towels, insecticide, and mold. As she unpacked, humming to herself, I stared out the window: a pirogue glided unhurriedly on the waveless water; the sky and the lake were welded together without a joint; a pale moon levitated in the haze. The sun was setting somewhere; everything was returning to darkness after an unhappy day out.

The ban on my wandering seemed to be suspended here; I left Sestra sprawling on her bed, happily attached to the Walkman. *Heart of Darkness* in hand, I took the uphill path going past other bungalows. I was hoping to escape dinner with my family; I needed to be elsewhere and alone. On the way from the airport they felt foreign to me, not unlike hired actors mindlessly performing gestures of care and kinship: Tata in his absurd pith helmet; Mama smirking, routinely scared of the future; Sestra approaching everything with useless curiosity—I could remember that I used to love them, but I could not remember why, and I was terrified.

The carefully trimmed hedges were moist with dusk; low, mushroomlike lanterns flickered by the path. I walked onto a terrace extending from a vast restaurant hall. At its center, like an altar, was a table laden with food and flowers. And there, with his back to me, picking slices of meat and chunks of fruit, mounting them on his plate, was Steve Spinelli. I recognized his triangular torso and narrow hips, his claw curls and cowboy boots. For a blink, I considered sneaking out, but then he turned—a veritable hillock of victuals on his plate—and looked at me with no surprise whatsoever.

"Look what the bitch dragged in," he said.

He walked out onto the terrace, and I went with him to his table; he offered me a seat and I took it, determined to leave as soon as possible, before Father caught me here. Without being asked, I said:

"We are going to Virunga National Park tomorrow, for a safari."

"It's a fun world, Blunderpuss," Spinelli said. "Getting funner every day."

"Is Natalie with you?"

"She is."

"Why are you here?"

He dug into the foodstuff with a spoon and chewed heartily with his mouth open, ignoring me. Between spoonfuls, he puffed on a cigarette, then put it back in the ashtray.

"For a vacation," he said. "And while I am here, I might as well discuss an important matter with your father."

"Like what?"

"You, maybe. Or maybe not. We'll burn that bridge when we get to it."

I grabbed his Marlboros and lit up. The possibility of a drug-laced cigarette crossed my mind, but it tasted good. He seemed to speak to me from a space in which no life mattered—all the roles and purposes had already been assigned, and I did not know what mine were. I fidgeted and tapped the ashes from my cigarette until the ember broke off.

"I hear that you are a good volleyball player," he said. "Did you like Antonyka?"

"How do you know him?"

"I know a lot of people. Anton is a remarkable gentleman, as well as a communist cocksucker."

He waved at Carlier, who was just walking into the restaurant hall accompanied by a tall man with sideburns and a scaphander Afro. Carlier spoke to the man brusquely, pointing at the meat tray, then at the flowers—there was some disorder to be redressed. "I know Carlier too, for example," Spinelli went on. "We used to run guns to Angola together." The tall man took notes, looking at Carlier with dismay, which tightened the muscles and sinews in his forearms. I envisioned him suddenly punching in Carlier's face, blood spraying onto his white shirt, Carlier falling to the ground and screaming for help.

"Your dad also played with you and Anton, didn't he?" Spinelli said. "I bet you played pretty good together."

Carlier left the tall man to deal with the problem at hand, and dropped into the chair next to Spinelli. He pulled a pipe out of his breast pocket, with his pinkie picked some detritus from its mouth, but didn't light it.

"Whipping would be too good for Monsieur Henri," Carlier said peevishly.

"One day, Carlier, he's gonna slit your throat," Spinelli said. "And I'll cry over your corpse till I can piss no more."

Scoffing with approbation, Carlier picked up my book, looked at it without interest, and put it down. I took it from his hand and bade them good night.

The mushroom lamps cast a feeble light on the path, but on nothing else. The lava gravel crunched under my feet. Obscure creatures rustled in the black trees and bushes. The sky was splattered with stars, smeared with the Milky Way. I was lost; I could not remember the number of my hut, identical to all the others; the path seemed to be a circle.

I don't know why I behaved like a lunatic. I heard footsteps coming down the path behind me; I stepped off into the darkness and ducked behind a tree with a precise clarity of action; somebody had already done it once and I was just repeating the exact motions. I dropped my book; whatever was concealed in the tree shuffled its way higher up, and I did not dare pick up the book. The tree bark was smooth and fragrant, my hand sweating against it. The footsteps stopped.

"Come out, Blunderpuss. I can see you."

I was afraid to move or look at him, exhaling to the end of my breath, then inhaling through my nostrils, getting airheaded and elated as if that were the way to make myself invisible. Something fell on my head from above—a leaf, an insect, monkey hair—but I did not brush it off. It was so easy here to forget everything, to lose all bearing. An army of insects screeched at a high, buzzing pitch, as though cutting through a steel cable; then they stopped. I stepped out on the path.

"Let's go and say hi to Monkeypie," Spinelli said. "She'd love to see you."

"Maybe later," I said. "I must go."

"She's crazy about you, you know. She talks about you all the time. She'd love to see you." He put his arm around my shoulders; I felt the weight of his forearm on my neck, as he softly pushed me forward.

Their room smelled of burnt sugar; the ceiling fan was dead. Natalie lay on her side, her hand tucked between the pillow and her cheek, a tranquil smile on her face lit by the bedside lamp. Around her biceps, a loose rubber rope twisted. On the nightstand were a syringe and a spoon and a burning candle. I was an instant behind myself: I saw what it all was, but the thought could not encrust itself with meaning. Spinelli caressed her forehead with the back of his hand and moved a stray hair from her cheek.

"She is beautiful, isn't she, so peaceful," he whispered. "Would you like to fuck her?"

"I don't know," I said. "I don't think so."

"She's a little out of touch, but she'd love it, believe me."

"No, thank you."

"What's your problem, Blunderpuss? When I was your age I had a hard-on twenty-four/seven."

He stood above her with his hands on his hips. I couldn't move, until my knees got so weak I sat down, my back to Natalie. In her oblivion, she did not budge when I leaned on her belly. I had reached the farthest point of navigation. *Dear Azra, the leaves have covered my path. I do not know if I will ever see you again.*

"You can't get it up, can you," he said, chortling. "You can't get it up. Let me show you something." He quickly unfastened his eagle-buckled belt and let his jeans drop down. His dick leapt at me and stood in my face like an erect cannon. Its head was perfectly purple; the blue veins seemed to be throbbing.

"A solid torpedo, and ready to explode," Spinelli said, and stroked it. "Do you wanna touch it? C'mon, touch it."

Natalie sighed but did not open her eyes; the candle flickered, nearly going out. With indescribable effort, I finally stood up and pushed him away. "Hey!" he said, stumbling backward with his pants at his ankles. Still, I expected him to grab me from behind as I was walking out, I was ready for him to smash my head against the door until I blacked out, but nothing happened.

Outside, a tremulous lightwake stretched itself toward the cataractous moon. My heart was playing the bridge from "Stairway to Heaven," but beyond the noise in my veins, beyond the limp limbs, beyond the cold-sweating skin, was a serene flow carrying me away from everything that had been me. Up the path, past an oddly azure pool with a school of insects drowning in it, I walked back toward the restaurant.

And at the restaurant there would be my family: my sister picking the green beans off Father's plate; Father slicing his steak, still wearing his pith helmet despite Mother's nagging; Mother parting the mashed potato and carrots on Sister's plate, because Sister never wanted them to touch. I would take my place at the table, and Father would ask me where I had been. Nowhere, I would say, and he would ask me nothing more. You'd better eat something, you look so pale, Mother would say. My sister would tell us how much she looked forward to our safari, to seeing the elephant and the antelope and the monkey. Tomorrow is going to be really great, she would cry, clapping with joy, I simply can't wait. And we would laugh, Mother, Father, and I, we would laugh, Ha, ha, ha, ha, ha, hiding desperately our rope burns.

Before I opened my eyes, I listened: Against the sound wall of a clattering train, two male voices; one of them was mine-deep and spoke with a southern Serbian accent; the other was mumbly and uttered words with the inflections of a Sarajevo thug, the soft consonants further softened, the vowels stuck in the gullet. I wasn't sure what they were talking about, but there was gurgling in the bottle neck, the crackling of a burning cigarette.

"France," the Sarajevan said.

"Refused entry."

"Germany."

"Refused entry."

"Greece."

"Never went."

"Refused entry."

"Got me there," the Serbian said, and chortled.

The train slowed to a stop; I heard the doors opening. One of the men got up and stepped out of the compartment; the other followed him. I opened my eyes; the doors slid shut. They pushed the window down and were smoking. A man and a woman ran toward the train, each with a couple of suitcases banging the sides of their calves—there was a gash in the woman's leg. I contemplated escaping from the compartment: I had a bundle of money and my life to worry

about. But my fellow travelers pressed their butts against the
door, the Y-crack peeping out of the pants of one of them.
The train lurched and started moving; they flicked their
cigarettes and came back in. I closed my eyes again.

"Did you know Tuka?" asked the Sarajevan.

"No."

"How about Fahro?"

"Which Fahro?"

"Fahro the Beast."

"Fahro the Beast. His nose was bitten off?"

"Yes, that Fahro."

"I didn't know him."

"Which cell block were you in?"

"Seven."

"Rape?"

"Burglary."

"Burglary was Six."

"Well, I was in Seven," the Serbian said, peevishly.

"I was in Five. Manslaughter."

"Nice."

"I was a little drunk."

"Life is death if you don't have a little drink every now
and then," concluded the Serbian wisely, and chugged from
the bottle. They fell silent, watching me. It was not unrea-
sonable to believe that they could smell my fear and were
just about to cut my throat and take the money. When I
sensed one of them shuffling his feet and moving toward
me, I opened my eyes. They were staring at me with bemused expressions.

"The child's awake," the Sarajevan said.

"Where are you headed?" the Serbian asked me.

"Zagreb," I said.

"What for?"

"To visit my grandfather."

"If Grandma had balls, she would be Grandpa," said the Sarajevan, for no apparent reason.

"Do you have a pretty sister we could be very nice to?" the Serbian asked, and licked his lips.

"No," I said.

My grandfather was dead, and when he was not, he did not live in Zagreb; I had a sister too. The truth was, my destination was Murska Sobota, I had a wad of money in my pocket, my mission to buy a freezer chest for my family.

Some weeks before I set out on this journey, my father had summoned a family meeting. "There arrives a time in the life of every family," he had said in his opening words, "when it becomes ready to acquire a large freezer chest." The ice box in the fridge was no longer spacious enough to contain the feed—meat, mainly—for the growing children; the number of family friends was so large that the supplies for an improvised feast had to be available at all times; "the well-being of our family requires new investments," abundance demanded more storage. My father used to like meetings like this, the family democracy game. We often had to sit through such a congress so we could vote on a decision he had already made. There were no objections this time either: my mother rolled her eyes at the rhetoric, even if she wanted a freezer chest; in the usual seventeen-year-old manner I made sure I was visibly indifferent; my sister was keeping notes, much too slowly. She was thirteen at the time, and still invested in the perfection of her handwriting.

But to my utter surprise, I was unanimously elected to be the purchaser of the freezer chest. Father worked in mysterious ways: he had tracked down the biggest chest—the six-hundred-liter model—available in the lousy market of socialist Yugoslavia; he somehow discovered that the best price was in Murska Sobota, a small town deep in Slovenia, not far from the Hungarian border. I was to take the night train to Zagreb, then a bus to Murska Sobota; I was to spend a night at the hotel ambitiously called Evropa; the next day I was to deliver the money to someone named Stanko, and that was where my mission ended. Stanko was to arrange the shipment, and all I needed to do was come back home safely.

The Sarajevan looked at me intently, possibly deciding whether to do me in because I obviously lied. He wore a suit and a tie, but his shoes looked shitty, the soles peeling off. Blinking very slowly, as if his eyes were counting time, he asked me:

"Do you fuck?"

"What?"

"Do you fuck? Do you use your dick the way it is supposed to be used?"

"A little," I said.

"I love to fuck," the Serbian said.

"There is nothing sweeter than a fuck," the Sarajevan said.

"Yeah," the Serbian said wistfully, and rubbed his crotch. He had tattooed knuckles; he wore a leather jacket and shoes so pointy that it seemed he had sharpened them so they could easily penetrate the skull.

Despite her voting for my deployment on the freezer-chest mission, my mother had worried about my traveling. I was excited: Murska Sobota sounded exotic and dangerous. This was the first time I would be away alone, on the road by myself, my first opportunity to live through experiences from which many a poem would spring. For I was a budding poet; I had filled entire notebooks with the verses of teenage longings and crushing boredom (always the flip side of longing). I equipped myself for the expedition: a fresh notebook; extra pencils; a book of Rimbaud's—my bible (*As I was floating down unconcerned Rivers / I no longer felt myself steered by the haulers* . . .); packs of Marlboros (rather than the usual crappy Drinas); and a single contraceptive pill I had gotten in exchange for *Physical Graffiti*, a double Led Zeppelin LP that I no longer cared about, as I had moved on to the Sex Pistols.

I was an unwilling virgin, my bones draped in amorous flesh. Consequently, I held a belief, not uncommon among adolescent males, that beyond the constraining circles of family, friends, and prudish high school girlfriends lay a vast, wild territory of the purest sex, where the merest physical or eye contact led to copulation unbound. I was ready for it: in preparation for the journey, I had tested a number of scenarios in my hormone-addled mind, determining that the crucial moment would be when I offered her the pill, thereby expressing my manly concern and gentlemanly responsibility—no female could say no to that.

"You look like a smart kid," the Sarajevan said. "Let's see if you can figure out this riddle."

"Let's hear it," the Serbian said.

"It has no head, but it has a hundred legs, a thousand windows, and five walls. It is never the same, but it is always almost the same. It is black and white and green. It disappears, and then it comes back. It smells of dung and straw and machine oil. It is the biggest thing in the world, but it can fit into the palm of your hand."

The Sarajevan watched me, wistfully stroking his three-day beard, as though remembering himself when he used to be my age, before he boarded the drunken boat of adulthood, before he knew the answer to the riddle.

"It's a house," the Serbian said.

"No house has a hundred legs, you stupid fuck," the Sarajevan said.

"Don't call me stupid," the Serbian said, and rose to face him, his hands rolled up into fists.

"All right, all right," the Sarajevan said, as he stood and embraced the Serbian. They hugged and kissed each other's cheeks several times, then sat down. I hoped the riddle was forgotten, but the Sarajevan would not let go; he poked my knee with his shitty shoe and said: "What is it, kid?"

"I don't know."

"An elephant," the Serbian said.

"Shut up," the Sarajevan said. The Serbian leapt up, ready for a punch; the Sarajevan got up; they embraced and kissed each other's cheeks; they sat down.

"Respect," the Serbian muttered. "Or I will crack your fucking skull open."

The Sarajevan ignored him. "What is it?" he asked me. I pretended I was thinking.

"Everything," the Serbian said. "It is everything."

"With all due respect, brother, that is probably not the correct answer."

"Who says?"

"Well, *everything* usually does not work as an answer to any riddle, and it does not disappear and come back."

"Says who?"

"Everybody knows that doesn't happen."

"I say it does."

"*Everything* cannot fit into the palm of your hand."

"I say it can," the Serbian said, and got to his feet, his fists clenched as tightly as ever. The Sarajevan stayed in his seat, shaking his head, apparently deciding against smashing the Serbian's face in.

"All right," he said, "if it is that important to you, it is everything."

"Because it is," the Serbian said, and then turned to me. "Isn't it?"

The blazing clarity of dawn: light creeping from beyond muddy fields; a plane leaving a white scar across the sky;

drunken soldiers howling songs of love and rape in the next compartment. The two men had quieted down, exhausted by their babbling, and I dropped off. When I woke up, they were gone, leaving the stench of sweaty mindlessness behind. I checked my pocket for the money, then wrote down the conversation and the riddle as I remembered them, and there were many other things to note. On this trip, I was happy to experience, everything was notable.

In Zagreb, I boarded a bus to Murska Sobota. The quaint hills of Zagorje, the picture-postcard houses and occasional fairy-tale castle mounted on a hillock; a healthy, well-dressed peasant leading a herd of healthy, fat cows across the horizon; chickens picking worms in the middle of a dirt road. I voraciously scribbled it all down—it seemed someone had cleaned and prettied up the land for my arrival. The man sitting next to me was invested in a crossword puzzle; he frowned and refrowned, fellating his pen. His cuffs were threadbare; his knuckles bruised; his ring stone was turned toward the middle finger. Many of his letters stretched beyond the little squares of the puzzle, the words curving up and down. At some point he turned his impeccably shaven face to me and asked, as though I were his assistant taking notes: "The biggest city in the world?" "Paris," I said, and he returned to the puzzle.

This happened in 1984, when I was long and skinny; my legs hurt, and I could not stretch them in the dinky bus. Pus accumulated in my budding pimples; there was an arbitrary erection in progress. This was youth: a perpetual sense of unease that made me imagine a place where my discomfort would be natural, where I could wallow in my wounds, in heavy air and sea. But my parents believed that it was their duty to guide me to a good, pleasant place where I could be normal. They arranged spontaneous conversations about my future, during which they insisted I declare what it was that I wanted, what my plans for life and college were. I responded with the derivations of Rimbaud's rants about the unknown quantity awakening in our era's universal soul, the soul encompassing everything: scents, sounds, colors, thought mounting thought, et cetera. Naturally, they were terrified with the fact that they had no idea what I was talking about. Parents know nothing about their children; some children lead their parents to believe that they can be understood, but it is a ruse—children are always one step ahead of their parents. My soul soliloquies often made Father regret that he hadn't belted me more when I was little; Mother secretly read my poetry—I found traces of her worried tears staining the pages of my notebooks. I knew that the whole purpose of the freezer-chest project was to confront me with what Father called "the laundry of life" (although Mother always did his laundry), to have me go through the banal, quotidian operations that constituted my parents' existence and learn that they were necessary. They wanted me to join the great community of people who made food collection and storage the central organizing principle of their life.

The food—bah! I forgot to touch the chicken-and-pepper sandwich my mother had made for me. In my notebook, I waxed poetic about the alluring possibility of simply going on, *into the infinity of lifedom*, never buying the freezer chest. I would go past Murska Sobota, to Austria, onward to Paris; I would abscond from the future of college and food storage; I would buy a one-way ticket to the utterly unforeseeable. Sorry, I would tell them, I had to do it, I had to prove that one could have a long, happy life without ever owning a freezer chest. *In every trip, a frightening, exhilarating possibility of never returning is inscribed. This is why we say good-bye*, I would write. *You knew it could happen when you sent me to the monstrous city, the endless night, when you sent me to Murska Sobota.*

I had never checked into a hotel before going to Murska Sobota. I worried about the receptionist at Hotel Evropa not letting me in because I was too young. I worried about not having enough cash, about my documents' being unexpectedly revealed as forged. I ran over the lines I was to deliver at the reception desk, and the rehearsal quickly turned into a fantasy in which a pretty receptionist checked me in with lassitude, then took me up to the room only to rip her hotel uniform off and submerge me into the wet sea of pleasure. The fantasy was duly noted in my notebook.

Needless to say, the receptionist was an elderly man, hairy and cantankerous, his stern name Franc. He was checking in a foreign couple, attired for traveling convenience in sneakers, khakis, and weatherproof jackets. They wanted something from him, something he wasn't willing to concede, and from their open vowels and nasal whining I recognized they were American. I didn't know then (and still don't know now) how to assess the age of human beings older than I, but the woman looked much younger than my mother, perhaps because of her smooth, unworked hands. Her husband was shorter than she, his wrinkles rippling away from his eyes, a dimple in his chin deep enough to put a screw in. He had both of his knuckly hands on the reception desk, as if about to mount it and charge at Franc, who was proudly bent on not smiling under any circumstances. As the woman kept shrilling, "Yeah, sure, okay," the receptionist kept shaking his head. He had a thin mustache closely tracing his upper lip, like a hair sediment. On his neck were parallel sets of sinister fingernail scratches.

I remember all this, even if I didn't write it down, because I spent an eternity waiting for the Americans to complete their check-in. I began imagining a conversation I would have with the woman, should we happen to share an elevator ride, while her unseemly husband was safely locked up somewhere in a distant reality. In my high school English, I would tell her that I liked her face flushed with pilgrimage, that I wanted to hold the summer dawn in my arms. We would stagger, embracing, to her room, where we wouldn't even make it to the bed, et cetera. Her name, I chose, was Elizabeth.

"Thank you," she finally said, and stepped away from the desk, her husband closely following her, as though blind.

"You're welcome," Franc said to their backs.

He had no interest in me, for I presented no challenge: he could speak Slovenian to me and not care whether I understood (I did); he could easily disregard any of my pipsqueak demands (he did). He took my ID and money, and gave me in return a large key attached to a wooden pear with "504" carved in it.

Elizabeth and her husband were still waiting for the elevator, talking in whispers. They glanced at me and did what Americans do when they make unnecessary, unwanted eye contact: they raise their eyebrows, roll their lips inward, and brighten up their face so it can bespeak innocent indifference. I said nothing, nor did I smile. On the pear that Elizabeth held I saw the number of their room, 505, and so when they stepped out, I followed them. My room was directly across from theirs, and as we entered our respective rooms, Elizabeth turned toward me and flashed a splendid smile.

It was in Murska Sobota that I truly confronted the ineluctable sadness of hotel rooms: a psyche with a notepad nobody had ever used to write; the bed cover with infernally purple flowers; a black-and-white picture of a soulless seaside resort; a garbage basket lined with crumpled paper tissues suggesting a messy quickie. The window looked over a concrete garage roof, in the middle of which was a vast puddle, shimmering like a desert-lake mirage. There was no way I was going to spend a night alone in this cave of sorrow. I needed to find places with a high density of youth, where comely Slovenian girls stood in clusters, steadily rejecting the clumsy advances of Slovenian boys, conserving their maidenhead for a pill-carrying Sarajevo boy, his body a treasure to squander.

The main street appeared to have been recently depopulated; only an occasional empty bus drove by, the lights in it dimmed. There were no cafés or bars or young people I could scout, only the windows of closed stores: stiffened mannequins, their arms opened in an obscure gesture of welcome; towers of concentric pots looming over families of pans; single shoes lined up closely on a rack, so different in sizes and shapes that each one of them seemed to represent a missing person. And there was the store I was to visit the next day to purchase for my family an entry into an abundant future. In the window, a humongous freezer chest glowed as if in a heavenly commercial.

I decided to explore the side streets and found nothing but a slumbering row of houses, the nightmarish murmur of television sets passing through a thousand quiet windows. Here and there, the sky was stained with stars. A neon sign in the distance announced the name of a bar called Bar, and there I went.

There was nobody in Bar except for a bearded, frog-faced man, whose chin was about to touch the brim of his beer stein, and a cloud of smoke hanging thick as a ghost. Without lifting his head, the man looked at me intently, as though he had been expecting me to arrive with a message of some sort. Message I had none, so I sat as far away from him as possible, close to the bar attended by nobody I could see. I lit a cigarette, determined to wait for female beauty to walk in.

The man lit up a cigarette too; he exhaled as though letting his soul out. I began thinking up a poem in which the main character walked into a bar as empty as this one, smoked and drank alone, thinking up wisecracks, and then, when he wanted to order another beer, discovered that the bartender was dead, slumped in a chair behind the bar, his left hand reaching for a stein of still-foaming beer. I had left my notebook in the hotel, so I could not write the poem down, but I kept thinking about it, kept coming up with rhymes, kept drinking my beer, kept not looking at the man. Most human lives perish without other people's ever noticing, and I recognized that it could happen to me too, tonight. They would find an uncomfortable corpse with a stack of cash and a mysterious pill and they would ask themselves: Where were we when he needed us? Why didn't we deflower him before he perished?

The man stood up and tottered toward me. The shoulders of his jacket almost reached his elbows, as though he had shrunk abruptly; a purple tie grew out of his shirt; he wore a little hat with a mangy feather stuck in its ribbon. He sat right across from me, mumbling a greeting. In the center of plum-colored circles his eyelids moved slowly, as though he was deciding each time whether to open his eyes at all. I turned back toward the bar, pretending to be looking for a bartender. The man grumbled and gibbered, pointing toward the bar, and I nodded understandingly. The sounds gradually attained the shape of complete sentences, punctuated by an occasional snort or a hand slamming the table. I could not figure out whether he was pissed or glad about my presence in his lair.

A waitress planted two large, foaming steins between us. She put a hand on my shoulder warmly, asking apparently if

I was okay. She was voluminous, her face seemed upholstered, her biceps doughy; she smelled of cakes and cookies. The drunk raised his stein and held it in front of me for a *cin-cin* until I complied. We drank and wiped foam off our lips with the back of our hands. He sighed in approval; I exhaled; we drank in silence and smoked.

More beer came. The man decided to open up to me: he leaned forward and back, he waved his hands in unintelligible derision, he pointed his finger in various directions, and then he started crying, tears streaming down his cheeks webbed with capillaries.

"Everything is okay," I said. "Everything will be fine." But he just shook his head, as there seemed to be no hope or relief. The waitress came over, unloaded more beer, and wiped his face with her dishrag; she appeared to be used to cleaning his tear-crusted cheeks. The man's tie was wet with tears; the beer parlor was dark and empty; I was drunk, muttering occasionally: "Everything will be fine." The waitress listlessly wiped glasses behind the bar; time passed in silence. *What will become of the world when you leave?* Rimbaud wrote. *No matter what happens, no trace of now will remain.* Then I started crying too.

I did not know how long it had all gone on, but when I left Bar, my sleeve was wet with tears and snot. I could recall the waitress wiping my face at least once with her rag stinking of rancid dishwater. I gave her what seemed to me a large chunk of the freezer-chest money and she locked the door behind me. The man stayed behind, his head carefully deposited on the clearing in the forest of steins—he probably lived there. And as I stepped out on the vacant streets of Murska Sobota, a wave of euphoria surged through me. This was *experience*: I had possibly lost my head and experienced a spontaneous outpouring of strong emotion; I had just drunk with a disgusting stranger, as Rimbaud surely did in Paris once upon a time; I had just said *Fuck the fuck off* to the responsible life my parents had in store for me; I had just spent time in the underworld of Murska Sobota and come out soaked with sweat and tears; I had a magic pill in my pocket. I needed somebody to love me tonight.

I found myself in a park infused with the dung-and-straw smell of budding trees and fledgling grass. At the center was a copper-green statue of a partisan with a rifle pointed toward the obscure treetops. A man in a fur hat held a leash under a weak light, while his Irish setter ran in circles with an imaginary friend, stopping every so often to look up hopefully at the man. The fur hat was the same auburn color as the dog, and for a moment I thought the man was wearing a dead puppy on his head. Just beyond the reach of light, a couple was groping, their hands stuck deep into each other.

I was giving up my hope of finding love, but across the empty street stood two young women, arm in arm, neatly clad in long coats. Their heels clacked as they crossed the street toward me; they giggled and chattered, their faces made up, their hair dewed with sourceless glimmer. One of them had a long narrow chin, the other had big dark eyes. They cut across the park at a brisk pace, avoiding the unlit edges. When they reached the brighter side of the street, I as well if he got hold of me. Oh, the horror of your body's not living up to the intensity of your fear—no matter how fast I wanted to run, my feet moved slowly, slipping a couple of times. I had visions of his pointed shoes breaking through my skin and skull and ribs. He abandoned the pursuit eventually, but I kept running.

Hotel Evropa emerged before me on a wholly unfamiliar street. Soaked to the bones, I savagely pushed and pulled the entrance door, until Franc, dreadfully hateful in the middle of his twenty-four-hour shift, unlocked it for me. I crept past him, focusing on each of my steps so as not to appear drunk. I pressed the elevator button and waited patiently, while my center of gravity rode the surf of my inebriation. I would have waited all night, for I did not want to exhibit my wobblibility, let alone ascend the eternal stairs to the fifth floor, but Franc barked at me that the elevator was already there—indeed, the door was wide open. I stepped into a sweat-tinged cloud of perfume and went up inhaling like a firefighter taking in oxygen.

The key would not enter the lock, no matter how hard I tried to push it in. Everything was wrong: I kicked the door with my knee, and then with my foot, and then again and again. Need I say it hurt? Need I say that the pain made everything much worse? Need I say that I was terrified out of my wits when I heard the lock turning and the door opened and there stood Elizabeth, loosely wrapped in a peignoir, pulling its flaps together to cover her uncoverable breasts. Her skin glowed of slumber, her tresses ruffled, she followed them, sticking to the dark side. They left the park and got on the main street, down which a cistern truck crawled, two men in tall rubber boots with snaky hoses in their hands washing the street. The asphalt glistened tarrishly, the women scuttering across the border between the wet and the dry. The strong stream from one of the hoses rushed toward my shoes and soaked them, so when I entered the dry territory, I left wet footprints behind.

Abruptly the two women stopped in front of the appliance store and examined my freezer chest, stolid and lit up. The narrow-chinned woman turned and looked at me, and in panic, I faced a travel agency window and a faded, crude collage of various exotic African landscapes, all photographed from high above. The women went on walking, quickening their pace until it matched the beating of my heart. It was impossible to stop now, for we were bound in this absurd pursuit. They turned the corner and I ran after them, feeling we might be reaching our goal.

Around the corner, they were standing with a man, all in denim, his large shovel-shaped hand comfortingly on their shoulders as they pointed at me, speaking to him with angry alacrity. He smiled and called me over, and for an insane instant I thought they were inviting me to party with them, but then he started unambiguously sprinting toward me. I took off at the speed of fear toward the hotel; I charged down the main street, splashing through puddles. Lighter than a cork, I danced forth on the waves. I did not dare turn to see where my pursuer was, but I heard his big feet hitting the ground steadily behind me. Those feet would hit me just smelled of dreams. "How can I help you?" is what she probably said. I probably said nothing or just groaned. Her husband was snoring so loudly that I thought he was faking it, the pitiful coward. She looked straight into my eyes; at the bottom of her eyes there was love, the only antidote to this vile despair. I wanted to hold her hand with rings like bejeweled palaces, I wanted to kiss her, I wanted her to leave her stertorous husband, deflower me, and cultivate me in the garden of my youth. All I needed to spark a conflagration of our heated bodies was the right move, the right word. So I said:

"Pill?"

"Excuse me?" she said.

I excavated the pill from my change pocket and offered it to her on the palm of my hand—it was tiny in the cut-out piece of packaging. She looked at it, baffled, then turned around as if to check whether her unwitting husband was still asleep.

"What is it, honey?" the husband cried. I quickly put the pill back in my pocket, as the husband was coming to the door. Elizabeth could see that I was mindful, that I was a considerate gentleman, young though I was. She flashed a barely perceptible smile and I understood we were in it together now, so when the husband came to the door, his pajamas baseball-patterned, his hair disheveled, I said, as innocently as I could, "Maybe you have pill? For head?" I pointed at my head, lest there be any confusion whose head we were talking about.

"No, I am sorry," Elizabeth said, and started closing the door, as I kept saying, "Maybe aspirin? One aspirin? Aspirin . . ."

She shut the door and locked it twice. Clearly, I had not said the right word; I was very drunk and had not considered this outcome. I thought that we had connected, that the electricity had started flowing between our trembling bodies. Swaying before the cruelly and unnecessarily closed door, I raised my hand to knock and clarify to Elizabeth that, yes, I was in love with her, and that, no, I didn't mind that she was married. I didn't do it; the door was closed as closed can be. I heard them murmuring conspiratorially, like a husband and wife, and I recognized that love was on the other side, and I had no access to it.

But the beauty of youth is that reality never quells desire, so when I unlocked my door I left it open, in case Elizabeth wanted to put her dull husband to sleep and then tiptoe over to my frolicsome den. Every now and then I peeped out, hoping to see her door slowly coming ajar, to see her lustfully scurrying over to me. Thus I was peering out when Franc strode out of the elevator, stopped at Elizabeth's door, gingerly knocked, as my jealous heart sank, and when she opened it, exchanged whispers with her. She pointed at me—for the last delusional moment I thought she had called him up to ask about me—and there I stood in the crack, grinning like a happy dog.

Franc charged over and pushed my door open, before I could lock it. With a flashing swing of his hand from his hip up to my face, he slapped me. My cheek burned, my eyes filled with fiery tears. I retreated toward the bed, until I stumbled and fell on the floor. Franc kicked me and kept kicking me: his shoes were pointed, and I felt the point sinking into my flesh, my buttocks and thighs, then hitting against my ribs and coccyx. I shrimped up and covered my face and head.

There was too much pain at that moment, my body numb and squandered; Franc's exertions and kicks were hysterical, therefore funny; the floor stank of machine oil. He didn't kick me in the face, as he could have done. He didn't spit on me, but on the floor next to me. He didn't yell at me, just snarled and growled, because the rapid fire of kicks was not easy on him; when he stopped, he was panting. Leaving, he calmly told me that if he were to hear a peepest peep from me, he would beat me to a pulp and pull me by my ears out onto the street, let the police have fun with me all night long. He was a good, if unpleasant, man, Franc was. He even slowly, carefully, closed the door.

I lay in the darkness, unable to move, until I fell asleep. The neon lights in the hall hummed; the elevator thudded going up, coming down. I dreamt of war, of might and right, of utterly unforeseeable logic. I woke up wishing I were home: there would have been the smell of French toast and my father's aftershave and the banana shampoo my sister liked to use. There would have been the weather forecast on the radio (my parents liked to know the future), my sister pouting because she couldn't listen to her music show. I would have walked in and derisively submitted myself to my mother's kiss. Breakfast would have been ready.

I stood up—the pain beginning to set in—and unpacked my mother's chicken-and-pepper sandwich; it was stale, the pepper mushy and bitter. I turned on the lights, found my notebook, and after biting into the sandwich and staring at the blank page for a long time, wrote a poem that I titled "Love and Obstacles," the first lines: *There are walls between the world and me, / and I have to walk through them.*

The following morning I woke up to find my body encrusted in dull, bruisey pain. I went to the store and delivered the money to Stanko. He had a scrubbing-wire beard, veins and sinews bulging on his hands as he counted and recounted the money. I was short a few dinars and told him that I had been robbed on the train; two brazen criminals had emptied my pockets, but had failed to find the rest of the money in my bag. Stanko stared at me until he believed me, then shook his head, appalled by the world that stole from its children. He made a note on the form before him, then showed me where to sign. He shook my hand earnestly and heartily, apparently congratulating me. When he offered me a cigarette, I took it and asked for another one. We smoked examining the freezer chest. Stanko seemed proud of it, as though he himself had created it. It was impressive: enormous, blazing white, and coffinlike in its emptiness; it smelled of clean, subzero death. It should come to us in two or three weeks, he said, and if it didn't, we should call him.

I slept on the bus and I slept on the night train, waking up only when my stomach started growling, when my body stiffened and started hurting again. I had no money to buy food, so I kept reliving the chicken-and-pepper sandwich and its beautiful smell. Dawn was descending upon earth; my compartment was freezing cold. I saw a horse grazing alone in a field, inexplicably wrapped in nylon; a copse of trees like toothpick tombstones; clouds on the horizon filled by an eternity of tears. When I arrived home, begrimed with having been away, breakfast was waiting.

The same day, Mother washed the denim pants I had worn in Murska Sobota, with the pill in the change pocket disintegrating—nothing was left except a nugget of foil and plastic. The freezer chest arrived after seventeen days. We filled it to the brim: veal and pork, lamb and beef, chicken and peppers. When the war began in the spring of 1992, and electricity in the city of Sarajevo was cut, everything in the freezer chest thawed, rotted in less than a week, and then finally perished.

The Conductor

In the 1989 *Anthology of Contemporary Bosnian Poetry,* Muhamed D. was represented with four poems. My copy of the anthology disappeared during the war, and I cannot recall the titles, but I do remember the subjects: one of them was about all the minarets of Sarajevo lighting up simultaneously at sunset on a Ramadan day; another was about the deaf Beethoven conducting his Ninth Symphony, unaware of the audience's ovations until the contralto touched his shoulder and turned him around. I was in my early twenties when the book came out, and compulsively writing poetry every day. I bought the anthology to see where I would fit into the pleiad of Bosnian poets. I thought that Muhamed D.'s poems were silly and fake; his use of Beethoven struck me as pretentious, and his mysticism as alien to my own rock 'n' roll affectations. But in one of the few reviews the anthology received, the critic raved, in syntax tortured on the rack of platitudes, about the range of Muhamed D.'s poetic skills and the courage he had shown in shedding the primitive Bosnian tradition for more modern forms. "Not only is Muhamed D. the greatest living Bosnian poet," the reviewer said, "he is the only one who is truly alive."

I had not managed to get any of my poetry published—nor would I ever manage—but I considered myself a far better, more soulful poet than Muhamed D. I had written about a thousand poems in less than two years, and occasionally I shored those fragments into a book manuscript that I sent to various contests. I can confess, now that I've long since stopped writing poetry, that I never really understood what I wrote. I didn't know what my poems were about, but I believed in them. I liked their titles ("Peter Pan and the Lesbians," "Love and Obstacles," et cetera), and I felt that they attained a realm of human innocence and experience that was unknowable, even by me. I delayed showing them to anyone else; I was waiting for readers to evolve, I suppose, to the point where they could grasp the vast spaces of my ego.

I met Muhamed D. for the first time in 1991, at a café called Dom pisaca, or Writers' Club, adjacent to the offices of the Bosnian Writers' Association. He was short and stocky, suddenly balding in his mid-forties, his expression frozen in an ugly permanent frown. I shook his hand limply, barely concealing my contempt. He spoke with the clear, provincial inflections of Travnik, his hometown, and was misclad in a dun shirt, brown pants, and an inflammable-green tie. I was a cool-dressed city boy, all denim and T-shirts, born and bred in the purest concrete, skipping vowels and slurring my consonants in a way that cannot even be imitated by anyone who did not grow up inhaling Sarajevo smog. He offered me a seat at his table, and I joined him, along with several of the other anthology veterans, who all wore the suffering faces of the sublime, as though they were forever imprisoned in the lofty dominion of poetry.

For some demented reason, Muhamed D. introduced

me to them as a philharmonic orchestra conductor. My objections were drowned out as the other poets started howling the "Ode to Joy" while making conducting gestures, and I was instantly nicknamed "Dirigent"—Conductor—thereby becoming safely and permanently marked as a nonpoet. I stopped trying to correct the mistake as soon as I realized that it didn't matter: it was my role to be only an audience for their drunken, anthological greatness.

Muhamed D. sat at the head of the Table, governing confidently as they babbled, ranted, sang heartbreaking songs, and went about their bohemian business, guzzling ambrosial beer. I occupied the corner chair, witnessing and waiting, dreaming up put-downs that I would never utter, building up my arrogance while craving their acceptance. Later that night, Muhamed D. demanded that I explain musical notation. "How do you read those dots and flags?" he asked. "And what do you really do with the stick?" Although I had no idea, I tried to come up with some reasonable explanations, if only to expose his ignorance, but he just shook his head in discouragement. Almost every night I spent at the Table, there was a point where I failed to enlighten the poets as to how music was written, thereby confirming their initial assumption that I was a lousy conductor, but a funny guy. I wondered how Muhamed D. could write a poem about Beethoven while being entirely oblivious of the way the damn notation system worked.

But the poets liked me, and I hoped that some of the pretty literature students who frequently served as their muses would like me too. I particularly fancied three of them: Aida, Selma, and Ljilja, all of whom pronounced soft consonants while pouting their moist lips, emitting energy that caused instant erections. I kept trying to get at least one of them away from the Table, so that I could impress her with a recitation of "Love and Obstacles." Not infrequently, I got sufficiently inebriated to find myself loudly singing a *sevdalinka*, sending significant glances toward the three muses, and emulating conducting moves for their enjoyment, while a brain-freezing vision of laying all three of them simultaneously twinkled on my horizon. But it never worked out: I couldn't sing, my conducting was ludicrous, I never recited any of my poems, I wasn't even published, and instead I had to listen to Muhamed D. singing his *sevdalinka* with a trembling voice that opened the worlds of permanent dusk, where sorrow reigned and the mere sight of a woman's neck caused maddening bouts of desire. The eyes of the literature muses would fill with tears, and he could pick whichever volunteer he chose to amuse him for the rest of the night. I'd totter home alone, composing a poem that would show them all that Muhamed D. had nothing on me, that would make Aida, Selma, and Ljilja regret never having let me touch them. I celebrated and sang myself on empty Sarajevo streets, and by the time I had unlocked the door and sneaked into my bed without waking up my poetry-free parents, I would have a masterpiece, so formidable and memorable that I would not bother to write it down. The next morning, I would wake up with my skin oozing a sticky alcoholic sweat and the sappy masterpiece gone forever from my mind. Then I would embark upon a furious series of unrhymed, anarchic poems, ridiculing Muhamed D. and the Table and the muses in impenetrably coded words, envisioning the devoted scholar who, one day, after decades of exploring my notes and papers, would decode the lines and recognize how tragically misunderstood and unappreciated I was. After writing all day, I'd head off to the Writers' Club and start the whole process again.

One night, Muhamed D. recited a new poem called "Sarajevo," which had two boys (*wisely chewing gum, / swallowing peppermint words*) walking the streets with a soccer ball (*They throw the ball through the snow, across Mis Irbina Street / as if lobbing a hand grenade across Lethe*). They accidentally drop the ball into the Miljacka, and the ball floats until it is caught in a whirlpool. They try to retrieve it with a device I had used once upon a time on my own lost ball: a crate is strung on a rope that stretches from bank to bank, and boys on either bank hold the ends of the rope, manipulating it until the ball is caught. Muhamed D. watches them from a bridge:

> *Whichever way I go, now, I'll reach the other shore.*
> *Old, I no longer know what they know: how to regain*
> *what is meant to be lost. On the river surface*
> *snowflake after snowflake perishes.*

He began his recitation in a susurrous voice, riding a tide of iambic throttles and weighted caesuras up to thunderous orgasmic heights, from where he returned to a whisper and then ceased altogether, his head bowed, his eyes closed. He seemed to have fallen asleep. The Table was silent, the muses entranced. So I said, "Fuck, that's old. What are you now—a hundred?" Uncomfortable with the silence, doubtless as jealous as I was, the rest of the Table burst out laughing, slapping their knees. I sensed the solidarity in mocking Muhamed, and for the first time I thought I would be remembered for something other than conducting—I would be remembered for having made Muhamed old. He smiled at me benevolently, already forgiving. But that very night, everybody at the Table started calling him "Dedo"— Old Man.

This took place just before the war, in the relatively rosy times when we were euphoric with the imminence of disaster—we drank and laughed and experimented with poetic forms into the late hours. We tried to keep the war away from the Table, but now and then a budding Serbian patriot would start ranting about the suppression of his people's culture, whereupon Dedo, with his newly acquired elder status, would indeed suppress him with a sequence of carefully arranged insults and curses. Inevitably, the nationalist would declare Dedo an Islamofascist and storm off, never to return, while we, the fools, laughed uproariously. We knew—but we didn't want to know—what was going to happen, the sky descending upon our heads like the shadow of a falling piano in a cartoon.

Around that time I found a way to come to the United States for a little while. In the weeks before I left, I roamed the city, haunting the territories of my past: here was a place where I had once stumbled and broken both of my index fingers; I was sitting on this bench when I first wedged my hand into Azra's tight brassiere; there was the kiosk where I had bought my first pack of cigarettes (Chesterfields); that was the fence that had torn a scar into my thigh as I was jumping it; in that library I had checked out a copy of *The Dwarf from a Forgotten Country* for the first time; on this bridge Dedo had stood, watching the boys recover the ball, and one of those boys could have been me.

Finally, I selected, reluctantly, some of my poems to show to Dedo. I met him at the Table early one afternoon, before everyone else arrived. I gave him the poems, and he read them, while I smoked and watched slush splash against the windows, then slide slowly down.

"You should stick to conducting," he said finally, and lit his cigarette. His eyebrows looked like hirsute little comets. The clarity of his gaze was what hurt me. These poems were told in the voice of postmodern Old Testament prophets, they were the cries of tormented individuals whose very souls were being depleted by the plague of relentless modernity. Was it possible, my poems asked, to maintain the reality of a person's self in this cruelly unreal world? The very inadequacy of poetry was a testimony to the disintegration of humanity, et cetera. But of course, I explained none of that. I stared at him with watery eyes, pleading for compassion, while he berated my sloppy prosody and the cold self-centeredness that was exactly the opposite of soul. "A poet is one with everything," he said. "You are everywhere, so you are never alone." Everywhere, my ass—the water dried in my eyes, and with an air of triumphant rationalism I tore my poetry out of his hands and left him in the dust of his neo-Romantic ontology. But outside—outside I dumped those prophetic poems, the founding documents of my life, into a gaping garbage container. I never went back to the Table, I never wrote poetry again, and a few days later I left Sarajevo for good.

My story is boring: I was not in Sarajevo when the war began; I felt helplessness and guilt as I watched the destruction of my hometown on TV; I lived in America. Dedo, of course, stayed for the siege—if you are the greatest living Bosnian poet, if you write a poem called "Sarajevo," then it is your duty to stay. I contemplated going back to Sarajevo early in the war, but realized that I was not and never would be needed there. So I struggled to make a living, while Dedo struggled to stay alive. For a long time, I didn't hear anything about him, and to tell the truth, I didn't really investigate—I had many other people to worry about, starting with myself. But news of him reached me occasionally: he signed some petitions; for one reason or another, he wrote an open letter to the pope; to an audience of annoyed Western diplomats he recited Herbert's "Report from the Besieged City" (*Too old to carry arms and fight like the others— / they graciously gave me the inferior role of chronicler*). Once I heard that he had been killed; a hasty paper even published an obituary. But it turned out that he had only been wounded—he had come back from the other side of Lethe with a bullet in his thigh—and he wrote a poem about it. The paper that published the obituary published the poem too. Predictably, it was called "Resurrection." In it, he walks the city as a ghost, after the siege, but nobody remembers him, and he says to them:

Can't you recall me? I am the one
Who carried upstairs your bloodied canisters,
Who slipped his slimy hand under the widow's skirt.
Who wailed the songs of sorrow,
Who kept himself alive when fools were willing to die.

Then he meets himself after the siege, *older than old*, and says to himself, alluding to Dante, *I did not know death hath undone so much*. It was a soul-rending poem, and I found myself hating him for it: he had written it practically on his deathbed, with no apparent effort, as his thigh wound throbbed with pus. I tried to translate it, but neither my Bosnian nor my English was good enough.

And he kept writing like a maniac, as though his resurrected life was to be entirely given over to poetry. Poems, mimeographed on coarse paper, bound in a frail booklet, were sent to me by long-unheard-from friends, carrying the smell (and microorganisms) of the many hands that had touched them on their way out of besieged Sarajevo. There were, naturally, images of death and destruction: dogs tearing at one another's throats; a boy rolling the body of a sniper-shot man up the street, much like Sisyphus; a surgeon putting together his wife's face after it has been blown apart by shrapnel, a piece of her cheek missing, the exact spot where he liked to plant his good-night kiss; clusters of amputated limbs burning in a hospital oven, the poet facing *the toy hell*. But there were also poems that were different, and I cannot quite define the difference: A boy kicks a soccer ball up so that it lands on the nape of his neck, and he balances it there; a young woman inhales cigarette smoke and holds it in as she smiles, everything stopping at that moment: *No tracing bullets lighting up the sky, / no pain in my riven thigh / no sounds*; a foreign conductor hangs on a rope, like a deft spider, over his orchestra playing the *Eroica* in a burnt-out building. I must confess that I believed for a moment that I was the conductor, that I was part of Dedo's world, that something of me remained in Sarajevo.

Still, living displaces false sentiments. I had to go on with my American life, keeping Dedo out of it, busying myself with local survival, getting jobs, getting into graduate school, getting laid. Every once in a while I unleashed the power of his words upon a sensitive American woman. The first one was Cheryl, the idle wife of a Barrington lawyer, whom I met at a Bosnian benefit dinner that she was kind enough to organize. At least one Bosnian was required to benefit from her benefit dinner, so she tracked me down through a friend, an expert in disability studies with whom I had read a paper at a regional MLA conference. Cheryl was generous beyond the dinner; before she went back to Barrington, I took her to my tiny studio—a monument to the struggles of immigration, with its sagging mattress, rotting shower curtain, and insomniac drummer next door. I recited Dedo's poems to her, pretending they were my own. She particularly liked the one about the man walking, during a lull in shelling, with his rooster on a leash, *a soul fastened to a dying animal.* Then I removed the permed tresses from her forehead so that I could kiss it and slowly undressed her. Cheryl writhed in my embrace, kissed me with clammy passion, hoisted her hips, and moaned with pleasure, as though the intensity of her orgasm would directly succor the Bosnian resistance. I could not help thinking, in the end, that she was fucking Dedo, for it was his words that had seduced her. But I took what was given and then rolled off into the darkness of my actual life.

After the charitable Cheryl, I was somewhat ashamed and for a while I could not stand to look at Dedo's poetry. I finished graduate school; I sold my stories; I was an author now. And somewhere along the way the war ended. On my book tour, I traveled around the country, reading to minuscule audiences, talking about Bosnia to a mixture of international relations and South Slavic languages students, simplifying the incomprehensible, and fretting all along that an enraged reader would stand up and expose me as a fraud, as someone who had no talent—and therefore no right—to talk about the suffering of others. It never happened: I was Bosnian, I looked and conducted myself like a Bosnian, and everyone was content to think that I was in constant, un-interrupted communication with the tormented soul of my homeland.

At one of those readings, I met Bill T., a professor of Slavic languages. He seemed to speak all of them, Bosnian included, and he was translating Dedo's latest book. With his red face, long, curly beard, and squat, sinewy body, Bill looked like a Viking. His ferocity was frightening, so I immediately flattered him by saying how immeasurably important it was to have Dedo's poetry translated into English. We went out drinking, and Bill T. drank like a true Viking too, while detailing the saga of his adventures in Slavic lands: a month with shepherds in the mountains of Macedonia; a year of teaching English in Siberia; his interviews with Solidarnosz veterans; the Slovenian carnival songs he had recorded. He had also spent some years, just for the hell of it, in Guatemala, Honduras, and Marrakech. The man had been everywhere, had done everything, and the drunker I got, the greater he was, and the more of nothing I had to say.

This was in Iowa City, I believe. I woke up the next morning on Bill T.'s sofa. My pants were laid out on the coffee table. Along the walls were dusty stacks of books. In the light fixture above me I could see the silhouettes of dead flies. A ruddy-faced boy with a gossamer mustache sat on the floor next to the sofa and watched me with enormous eyes.

"What are you doing here?" the boy asked calmly.

"I don't really know," I said, and sat up, exposing my naked thighs. "Where is Bill?"

"He stepped out."

"Where is your mom?"

"She's busy at the moment."

"What is your name?"

"Ethan."

"Nice to meet you, Ethan."

"Likewise," Ethan said. Then he grabbed my pants and threw them at me.

It was while I was slouching down the linden-lined street, where people nodded at me from sunny porches and able-bodied squirrels raced up and down the trees—it was then that the story Bill had told me the night before about Dedo fully hit me and I had to sit down on the curb to deal with it.

Dedo had come to Iowa City, Bill said, to be in the International Writing Program for twelve weeks. Bill had arranged it all, and volunteered to put Dedo up in the room above his garage. Dedo arrived with a small duffel bag, emaciated and exhausted, with the English he picked up while translating Yeats and a half-gallon of Jack Daniel's he picked up in a duty-free shop. The first week, he locked himself in above the garage and drank without pause. Every day, Bill knocked on the door, imploring him to come out, to meet the dean and the faculty, to mingle. Dedo refused to open the door and eventually stopped responding altogether. Finally, Bill broke the door down, and the room was an unreal mess: Dedo had not slept in the bed at all, and it was inexplicably wet; there were monstrous, bloody footprints everywhere, because Dedo had apparently broken the Jack Daniel's bottle, then walked all over it. A box of cookies had been torn open and the cookies were crushed but not eaten. In the trash can were dozens of Podravka liver pâté cans, cleaned out and then filled with cigarette butts. Dedo was sleeping on the floor in the corner farthest from the window, facing the wall.

They subjected him to repeated cold showers; they cleaned him up and aired out the room; they practically force-fed him. For another week he wouldn't stick his nose out of the room. And then, Bill said, he began writing. He did not sleep for a week, delivering poems first thing in the morning, demanding translations by the afternoon. "American poets used to be like that," Bill said wistfully. "Now all they do is teach and complain and fuck their students on the sly."

Bill canceled his classes and set out to translate Dedo's poems. It was like entering the eye of a storm every day. In one poem, Bill said, a bee lands on a sniper's hand, and he waits for the bee to sting him. In another one, Dedo sees an orange for the first time since the siege began, and he is not sure what is inside it—whether oranges have changed during his time away from the world; when he finally peels it, the smell inhales him. In another, Dedo is running down Sniper Alley and a woman is telling him that his shoe is untied, and with a perfect clarity of purpose, with the ultimate respect for death, he stoops to tie it, and the shooting ceases, for even the killers appreciate an orderly world. "I could not believe," Bill said, "that such things could come out of that pandemonium."

At the end of the third week Dedo gave a reading. With a mug of Jack at hand he barked and hissed his verses at the audience, waving a shaky finger. After he had read, Bill came out and read the translations slowly and serenely in his deep Viking voice. But the audience was confused by Dedo's hostility. They clapped politely. Afterward, faculty and students came up to him to ask about Bosnia and invite him to luncheons. He visibly loathed them. He livened up only when he realized that he had a chance to lay one of the graduate students who was willing to open her mind to "other cultures." He was gone the next week, straight back to the siege, sick of America after less than a month.

In the years after the war, only the occasional rumor reached me: Dedo had survived a massive heart attack; he'd made a deal with his physician that he would stop drinking but go on smoking; he'd released a book based on conversations with his young niece during the siege. And then—this made the news all over Bosnia—he'd married an American lawyer, who was working in Bosnia collecting war-crime evidence. The newspapers cooed over the international romance: he had wooed her by singing and writing poetry; she had taken him to mass grave sites. A picture from their wedding showed her to be a foot taller than he, a handsome woman in her forties with a long face and short hair. He consequently produced a volume of poems, titled *The Anatomy of My Love*, featuring many parts of her remarkably healthy body. There were poems about her instep and her heel, her armpit and her breasts, the small of her back and the size of her eyes, the knobs on her knees and the ridges on her spine. Her name was Rachel. I heard that they had moved to the

United States—following her body, he had ended up in Madison, Wisconsin.

But I do not want to give the impression that I thought about him a lot or even often. The way you never forget a song from your childhood, the way you hear it in your mind's ear every once in a while—that's how I remembered him. He was well outside my life, a past horizon visible only when the sky of the present was particularly clear.

As it was on the cloudless morning of September 11, 2001, when I was on a plane to D.C. The flight attendant was virginally blond. The man sitting next to me had a ring of biblical proportions on his pinkie. The woman on my right was immensely pregnant, squeezed into a tight red dress. I, of course, had no idea what was going on—the plane simply landed in Detroit and we disembarked. The Twin Towers were going down simultaneously on every screen at the unreal airport; maintenance personnel wept, leaning on their brooms; teenage girls screamed into their cell phones; forlorn pilots sat at closed gates. I wandered around the airport, recalling the lines from Dedo's poem: *Alive, I will be, when everybody's dead. / But there will be no joy in that, for all those / undone by death need to pass / through me to reach hell.*

While America settled into its mold of patriotic vulgarity, I began to despair, for everything reminded me of Bosnia in 1991. The War on Terror took me to the verge of writing poetry again, but I knew better. Nevertheless, I kept having imaginary arguments with Dedo, alternately explaining to him why I had to write and why I should not write poetry, while he tried to either talk me out of writing or convince me that it was my duty. Then, last winter, I was invited to read in Madison and hesitantly accepted. Dedo was the reason for both the hesitation and the acceptance, for I was told that he would be one of the other readers.

So there I was, entering the large university auditorium. I recognized Dedo in the crowd by his conspicuous short-ness, his bald dome reflecting the stage lights. He was changed: he'd lost weight; everything on him, from his limbs to his clothes, seemed older and more worn; he wiped his hands on his corduroy pants, nervously glancing up at the people around him. He was clearly dying to smoke, and I could tell that he was not drunk enough to enjoy the spot-light. He was so familiar to me, so related to everything I used to know in Sarajevo: the view from my window; the bell of the dawn streetcar; the smell of smog in February; the shape that the lips assume when people pronounce their soft Slavic consonants.

"Dedo," I said. "*Šta ima?*"

He turned to me in a snap, as if I had just woken him up, and he did not smile. He didn't recognize me, of course. It was a painful moment, as the past was rendered both imagi-nary and false, as though I had never lived or loved. Even so, I introduced myself, told him how we used to drink together at the Writers' Club; how he used to sing beautifully; how often I remembered those times. He still couldn't recall me. I proceeded with flattery: I had read everything he'd ever written; I admired him, and as a fellow Bosnian, I was so proud of him—I had no doubt that a Nobel Prize was around the corner. He liked all that and nodded along, but I still did not exist in his memory. I told him, finally, that he used to think I was a conductor. *"Dirigent!"* he exclaimed, smiling at last, and here I emerged into the light. He embraced me, awkwardly pressing his cheek against my chest. Before I could tell him that I had never conducted and still was not conducting, we were called up to the stage. He had a rotten-fruit smell, as if his flesh had fermented; he went up the stairs with a stoop. Onstage, I poured him a glass of ice water, and instead of thanking me, he said, "You know, I wrote a poem about you."

I do not like reading in front of an audience, because I am conscious of my accent and I keep imagining some American listener collecting my mispronunciations, giggling at my muddled sentences. I read carefully, slowly, avoiding dialogue, and I always read the same passage. Often, I do it like a robot—I just read without even thinking about it, my lips moving but my mind elsewhere. So it was this time: I felt Dedo's gaze on my back; I thought about his mistaken memories of me conducting a nonexistent orchestra; I wondered about the poem that he had written about me. It could not have been the poem with the spider-conductor, for surely he knew that I was not in Sarajevo during the siege. Who was I in his poem? Did I force the musicians to go beyond themselves, to produce sublime beauty on mistuned instruments? What were we playing? Beethoven's Ninth? *The Rite of Spring? Death and Transfiguration?* I sure as hell was not conducting the Madison audience well. They applauded feebly, having all checked out after the first paragraph or so, and I feebly thanked them.

"Super," Dedo said when I crawled back into my seat, and I could not tell whether he was being generous or whether he just had no idea how bad it really was.

Dedo was barely visible behind the lectern. Bending the microphone down like a horribly wilted flower, he announced that he was going to read a few poems translated into English by his "angel wife." He started from a deep register; then his voice rose steadily until it boomed. His vowels were flat, no diphthongs audible; his consonants were hard, maximally consonanty; the*s were duh*s; no *r*'s were rolled. His accent was atrocious, and I was happy to discover that his English was far worse than mine. But the bastard scorched through his verses, unfettered by self-consciousness. He flung his arms like a real conductor; he pointed his finger at the audience and stamped his foot, leaning toward and away from the microphone, as two young black women in the first row followed the rhythm of his sway. Then he read as if to seduce them, whispering, slowly:

Nobody is old anymore—dead or young, we are.
The wrinkles straighten up, the feet no longer flat.
Cowering behind garbage containers, flying away
from the snipers, everybody is a gorgeous body
stepping over the corpses, knowing:
We are never as beautiful as now.

Later I bought him a series of drinks at a bar full of Badgers pennants and kids in college-sweatshirt uniforms, blaring

TVs showing helmeted morons colliding head-on. We huddled in the corner, close to the toilets, and drank bourbon upon bourbon; we exchanged gossip about various people from Sarajevo: Sem was in D.C., Goran in Toronto; someone I knew but he could not remember was in New Zealand; someone I had never known was in South Africa. At a certain point he fell silent; I was the only one talking, and all the suppressed misery of living in America surged from me. Oh, how many times I had wished death to entire college football teams. It was impossible to meet a friend without arranging a fucking appointment weeks in advance, and there were no coffee gardens where you could sit and watch people walk by. I was sick of being asked where I was from, and I hated Bush and his Jesus freaks. With every particle of my being I hated the word "carbs" and the systematic extermination of joy from American life, et cetera.

I don't know whether he heard me at all. His head hung low and he could have been asleep, until he looked up and noticed a young woman with long blond hair passing on her way to the toilet. He kept his gaze on her backpack, then on the toilet door, as if waiting for her.

"Cute," I said.

"She is crying," Dedo said.

We went to another bar, drank more, and left after midnight. Drunk out of my mind, I slipped and sat in a snow pile. We laughed, choking, at the round stain that made it seem as if I had soiled my pants. The air was scented with burnt burgers and patchouli. My butt was cold. Dedo was drunk too, but he walked better than I, skillfully avoiding tumbles. I do not know why I agreed to go home with him to meet his wife. We wobbled down quiet streets, where the trees were lined up as if dancing a quadrille. He made me sing, and so I sang: *Put putuje Latif-aga / Sa jaranom Sulej-manom.* We passed a house as big as a castle; a Volvo stickered with someone else's thought; Christmas lights and plastic angels eerily aglow. "How the fuck did we get here?" I asked him. "Everywhere is here," he said. Suddenly he pulled a cell phone out of his pocket, as if by magic—he belonged to a time before cell phones. He was calling home to tell Rachel that we were coming, he said, so that she could get some food ready for us. Rachel did not answer, so he kept redialing.

We stumbled up the porch, past a dwarf figure and a snow-covered rocking chair. Before Dedo could find his keys, Rachel opened the door. She was a burly woman, with austere hair and eventful earrings, her chin tucked into her underchin. She glared at us, and I have to say I was scared. As Dedo crossed the threshold, he professed his love to her with an accent so horrible that I thought for an instant he was kidding. The house smelled of chemical lavender; a drawing of a large-eyed mule hung on the wall. Rachel kept saying nothing, her cheeks puckering with obvious fury. I was willing now to give my life for friendship—I might have abandoned him in Sarajevo, but now we were facing Rachel together.

"This is my friend, Dirigent," he said, propping himself up on his toes to land a hapless kiss on her taut lips. "He is conductor." I made ridiculous conducting moves, as if to prove that I could still do it. She didn't even look at me; her eyes were pinned on Dedo.

"You're drunk," she said. "Again."

"Because I love you," he said. I nodded.

"Excuse us," she said, and pulled him deeper into the house, while I stood in the hallway deliberating over whether to take my shoes off. A little ball of dust moved down the hall, away from the door, like a scared dog. I recalled Dedo's poem about the shoes he had bought the day before the siege started, which he would never wear, for *they get dirty on the streets filthy with death.* Every day he polished his new shoes with what could be his last breath, *hoping for blisters.*

He emerged from the house depths and said, "*Daj pomozi*"—Help me.

"Get the hell out, you drunken pig," Rachel snarled in his wake. "And take your stupid friend with you."

I decided not to remove my shoes and, stupidly, said, "It's O.K."

"It is not O.K.!" Rachel shouted. "It has never been O.K. It will never be O.K."

"You must be nice to him," Dedo screamed at her. "You must respect."

"It's O.K," I said.

"Not O.K. Never O.K. This is my friend." Dedo stabbed himself with his stubby finger. "Do you know me? Do you know who am I? I am biggest Bosnian poet alive."

"He is the greatest," I said.

"You're a fucking midget, is what you are!" She leaned

into him, and I could see his pointed-finger hand unfolding and swinging for a slap.

"Come on, midget," Rachel bellowed. "Hit me. Yeah, sure. Hit me. Let's have Officer Johnson for coffee and cookies again."

Detergentlike snow had already covered our footprints. We stood outside on the street, Dedo fixated on the closed door, as though his gaze could burn through it, cursing in the most beautiful Bosnian and listing all her sins against him: her bastard son, her puritanism, her president, her decaf coffee. Panting, he bent over and grabbed a handful of snow, shaped it into a frail snowball, and threw it at the house. It disintegrated into a little blizzard and sprinkled the dwarf's face. He was about to make another wretched snowball when I spotted a pair of headlights creeping down the street. It looked like a police vehicle, and I did not want to risk coffee and cookies with Officer Johnson, so I started running.

Dedo caught up to me around the corner, and we staggered down an alley in an unknown direction: the alley was deserted except for a sofa with a stuffed giraffe leaning on it. There were weak tire-mark gullies and fresh traces of what appeared to be a three-legged dog. We saw a woman in the kitchen window of one of the nearby houses. She was circling around something we could not see, a glass full of red wine in her hand. The snow was ankle-deep; we watched her, mesmerized: a long, shiny braid stretched down her back. The three-legged dog must have vanished, for the prints just stopped in the middle of the alley. We could go neither forward nor back, so we sat down right there. I felt the intense pleasure of giving up, the expansive freedom of utter defeat. *Whichever way I go, now, I'll reach the other shore.* Dedo was humming a Bosnian song I didn't recognize, snowflakes melting on his lips. It was clear to me that we could freeze to death in a Madison back alley—it would be a famous way to die. I wanted to ask Dedo about the poem he had written about me, but he said, "This is like Sarajevo in 'ninety-three." Perhaps because of what he had said, or perhaps because I thought I saw Officer Johnson's car passing the alley, I got up and helped him to his feet.

In the cab, it was only a question of time before someone vomited. The Arab cabbie despised us, but Dedo tried to tell him that he was a fellow Muslim. Madison was deserted.

"You are my brother," Dedo said, and squeezed my hand. "I wrote a poem about you."

I tried to kiss his cheek, as the cabbie glared at us in the rearview mirror, but awkwardly managed only to leave some saliva on his forehead.

"I wrote a good poem about you," Dedo said again, and I asked him to tell it to me.

He dropped his chin to his chest. He seemed to have passed out, so I shook him, and like a talking doll, he said, "He whips butterflies with his baton. . . ." But then we arrived at my hotel. Dedo kept reciting as I paid for the cab, and I didn't catch another word.

I dragged him to the elevator, his knees buckling, the snow thawing on his coat, releasing a closet-and-naphthalene smell. I could not tell whether he was still reciting or simply mumbling and cursing. I dropped him to the floor in the elevator and he fell asleep. He sat there in a pile, while I was unlocking the door to my room, and the elevator closed its doors and took him away. The thought of his being discovered in the elevator, drooling and gibbering, gave me a momentary pleasure. But I pressed the call button, and the elevator carrying Dedo obediently came back. *We are never as beautiful as now.*

The crushing sadness of hotel rooms; the gelid lights and clean notepads; the blank walls and particles of someone else's erased life: I rolled him into this as if into hell. I hoisted him onto the bed, took off his shoes and socks. His toes were frostbitten, his heels brandished a pair of blisters. I peeled off his coat and pants, and he was shivering, his skin goose-bumped, his navel hidden in a hair tuft. I wrapped the bed-covers around him and threw a blanket on top. Then I lay down next to him, smelling his sweat and infected gums. He grunted and murmured, until his face calmed, the eyelids smoothing into slumber, the brows unfurrowing. A deep sigh, as when dusk falls, settled in his body. He was a beautiful human being.

And then on Tuesday, last Tuesday, he died.

Good Living

B ack in the days of the war in Bosnia, I was surviving in Chicago by selling magazine subscriptions door-to-door. My employers thought that my Bosnian accent, clearly manufactured in the nether area of "other cultures," was quirky, and therefore stimulant to the shopping instincts of suburban Americans. I was desperate at the time, what with the war and displacement, so I shamelessly exploited any smidgen of pity I could detect in lonely housewives and grumpy retirees whose doors I knocked at. Many of them were excited by my very presence at their doorstep, as I was living evidence of the American dream: here I was, over-coming adverse circumstances in a new country, much like the forebears of the future subscriber, presently signing the check and wistfully relating the saga of the ancestral transi-tion to America.

But I had much too much of a dramatic foreign accent for the prime subscription-selling turf of the North Shore suburbs, where people, quaintly smothered by the serenity of wealth, regularly read *Numismatic News* and bought a life-time subscription to *Life Extension*. Instead, I was deployed in the working-class suburbs, bordering with steel-mill com-plexes and landfills, and populated with people who, unlike the denizens of the North Shore, did not think that I coveted what they had, because they did not exactly want it themselves.

My best turf was Blue Island, way down Western Avenue, where addresses had five-digit numbers, as though the town was far back of the long line of people waiting to enter downtown paradise. I got along pretty well with the Blue Islanders. They could quickly recognize the indelible lousiness of my job; they offered me food and water; once I nearly got laid. They did not waste their time contemplating the purpose of human life; their years were spent as a tale is told: slowly, steadily, approaching the inexorable end. In the meantime, all they wanted was to live, wisely use what little love they had accrued, and endure life with the anesthetic help of television and magazines. I happened to be in their neighborhood to offer the magazines.

A smokestack of the garbage incinerator, complete with sparks flying upward, loomed over the town like a church spire. Perhaps that was why the deciduous leaves in Blue Island died so abundantly and beautifully, its streets thickly covered with yellow, orange, ocher, russet layers. One day I walked over a dry carpet of honey-colored leaves, up to a dusty porch littered with disintegrating sheets of coupons. A brushy black cat did not move as I walked by; a wooden figure of the Virgin Mary hung stiffly by the bell. Someone shouted, "Come in!" before I rang, and in I walked, into a cavernous dark room reeking of overcurdled milk and beeswax tapers. On the couch, in its center, sat a small priest— the solemn attire, the white collar, the silver-cross pendant—his toy feet barely reaching the floor. His face and bald dome were blighted with red blotches and flaking skin. In his right hand he had a glass of Scotch, the half-empty bottle on the coffee table in front of him surrounded by the rubble of newspapers and snack bags. On his potbelly ledge, around the cross, there were potato-chip crumbles.

"What can I do you for?" he said, and belched. "Excuse me. What can I do for you?" He pointed at the armchair across the coffee table, so I sat down.

A salesman's job consists largely of mindless repetition of prefabricated phrases. Thus I offered him a wide selection of magazines that covered all areas of contemporary living. There was a magazine for everyone, whether his interest be in astronomy or self-betterment or gardening. I could also offer a wide variety of titles for a contemporary Christian reader: *Christianity Today, Christian Professional, God's Word Today* . . .

"Where're you from?" he asked, and took a large sip from the glass. The color of the Scotch rhymed with the leaves outside.

"Bosnia."

"Be not forgetful to entertain strangers," he slurred, "for thereby some have entertained angels unawares."

I nodded and suggested a few magazines that would open new horizons for him in archaeology or medicine or science. He shook his head, frowning, as though he could not believe in my existence.

"Have you lost anyone close to you in the war? Anyone you loved?"

"Some," I said, and lowered my head, suggesting intense soul pain.

"It must have been hard for you."

"It hasn't been easy."

Abruptly he turned his head toward the dark door in the back of the room and yelled: "Michael! Michael! Come here and see someone who is really suffering. Come and meet an actual human being."

Michael stepped into the room buttoning up, the impeccably white shirt closing in on a chest smooth and hairless. He was blond and blue-eyed, incongruously handsome in the Blue Island dreariness, sporting the square jaw of the American movie star.

"The young man here is from Bosnia. Do you have any idea where Bosnia is, Michael?"

Michael said nothing and strolled over to the coffee table, throwing his shoulders model-like. He dug up a cigarette from the coffee table wreckage and walked out, leaving a wake of anger behind.

"He smokes," the priest said, plaintively. "He breaks my heart."

"Smoking is bad," I said.

"But he works out a lot," the priest said. "Absent in spirit, but present in body."

I had a selection of magazines just for Michael, I said. *Men's Health, Shape, Self, Body + Soul,* all of them covering a wide range of interests: workout regimens, fitness tips, diets, et cetera.

"Michael!" the priest hollered. "Would you like a subscription to *Body and Soul*?"

"Fuck you," Michael screamed back.

The priest finished his Scotch and pushed himself awkwardly up from the couch to reach the bottle. I was tempted to help him.

"If there were a magazine called *Selfishness*," he grumbled, "Michael would be editor in chief."

He refilled the glass and returned into the depth of the couch. He scratched his dome and a flock of skin flakes fluttered up in its orbit.

"Michael wants to be an actor, you see. He is nothing if not vanity and vexation," the priest said. "But he has only managed to be a fluffer in the odd adult movie. And to tell you the truth, I cannot see a future in fluffing for him."

It was time for me to go. I was experienced enough to recognize the commencement of an unsolicited confession. I had stood up and left in the middle of a confession before—no doubt adding to the confessor's flow of tears—because it had been the prudent thing to do. But this time I could not leave, perhaps because the drama was titillatingly unresolved, or because the priest was so minuscule and weak, whole parchments peeling off his forehead. Having been often pitied, I savored pitying someone else.

"I've known Michael since he was a boy. But now he thinks he can go off on his own. It is not good that the man shall be alone, it is not good."

Michael appeared out of the room in the back, his hair

immaculately combed but still quivering in exasperation. He stormed past us and left the house, slamming the door behind him.

The priest finished off the Scotch in the glass in one big gulp.

"We all do fade as a leaf," he said, and threw the glass toward the coffee table. It dropped on top of the mess, and rolled down, off the table, out of sight. It was time for me to go; I started getting up.

"Do you know who Saint Thomas Aquinas was?" he said, raising his finger, as though about to preach.

"Yes, of course I know," I said.

"When he was a young man, his family did not want him to devote his life to the church, so they sent a beautiful maiden to tempt him out of it. And he chased her away with a torch."

He stared at me for a very long moment, as though waiting for a confirmation of my understanding, but it never came—understanding was not my job.

"Be not righteous overmuch," he said, fumbling the word "overmuch." "I never had a torch."

The door flung open and Michael charged back in. I sank into the chair, as he walked to the priest and stood above him, pointing his index finger at him, shaking it, his jaw jutted sideways with fury.

"I just want to say one thing, you sick fuck," he said, a few loose hairs stuck to his sweaty brow. "I just want to say one more thing to you."

We waited in the overwhelming silence, the priest closing his eyes, anticipating a punch. But Michael could not think of one more thing to say, so he finally said nothing, turned on his heel, and marched out, not bothering to slam the door this time. The priest grabbed a couch pillow and started banging it against his forehead, howling and hissing in pain. I took the opportunity to slither toward the open door.

"Wait," he wailed. "I want to subscribe. I want subscription. Wait a minute."

So I signed him up for two plum two-year subscriptions. His name was Father James McMahon. For the rest of the evening, I went around the neighborhood telling everybody—the old ladies, the young mothers, the cranky ex-policemen—that Father McMahon had just subscribed to *American Woodworker* and *Good Living*, wouldn't you know it? A few asked me how he seemed to be doing, and I would tell them that he had had a big fight with his young friend. And they would sigh and say, "Is that so?" and frown and subscribe to *Creative Knitting* and *FamilyFun*. It was by far my best day as a magazine salesman. At the end of the shift, waiting to be picked up by the turf manager, I watched the flickering TV lights in the windows and the sparkling stars up in the sky, and I thought: I could live here. I could live here forever. This is a good place for me.

Szmura's Room

He stands at Szmura's door, his left hand suspended in midair, reluctant to knock. Flanked by two suitcases, one of which is held together by a frayed rope, he palpitates, out of shape and undernourished. He is clad in a dark coat, the collar striated with lint and dandruff, the sleeves tragicomically short, exposing his dirt-rimmed shirt cuffs. When Mike Szmura opens the door, wearing nothing but pajama bottoms and a front of frightening chest hair, Bogdan utters his lines in stuttering English. "Right off the boat," Szmura says in a maliciously nasal voice. He steps aside to let our boy enter the apartment, the roped suitcase banging at his ankles, the other one smashing against Szmura's knee.

At least, that is how Szmura described it to us later, exhibiting the obscure alleged bruise on his knobby knee. We had interrupted our poker game (my two jacks were waiting to lure Szmura and Pumpek into surrendering their weekly income) so that Szmura could use his meager narrative talents to depict and embellish Bogdan's arrival. The other players, Pumpek and a couple of realtor buddies he brought along to serve as suckers, were unabashedly American and uninterested, and they impatiently waited for Szmura to finish so the game could go on. But in a likely attempt to distract me from the game, Szmura added, "He is from your lousy country, *Basnia*, whatever you call it." My two jacks promptly responded to the insult, and by the time I had raked in the loot with both hands, I had forgotten all about the forlorn foreigner at Szmura's door.

At subsequent poker games I learned more. Szmura attempted to entertain us with a repertoire of dumb-foreigner acts and bad-accent jokes featuring Bogdan, and from these performances, I gathered that Bogdan was much like me, an oddity: a Ukrainian from Bosnia, although, unlike me, he was not from Sarajevo. Szmura had no interest in internal Bosnian cultural differences and presupposed that there was a deep, essential kinship between us, which is to say that by mocking Bogdan he was making me the target. I preferred taking his money to taking exception—he had reached the point of writing promissory notes, and I kept them, as if they were love notes, even after he'd made good on them.

Bogdan had been delivered to Chicago through some lamentably narrow refugee channel—a Uke priest knew a Uke priest who knew about a cheap room at Szmura's. The size of a closet, the room was in the apartment that Szmura rented from his ex-girlfriend's grandmother, who blissfully chose to ignore the fact that Szmura had permanently and irreversibly dumped the apple of her eye shortly after banging her.

As small as the room was, it echoed with emptiness. Bogdan parked his suitcases flat in the windowless corner; took a sheet and a blanket out of the unroped one and spread them under the murky window—unequipped with mattress or duvet, this was where he would sleep. The room resembled an installation in a vacuous art gallery, the reflection of the ceiling bulb on the wood floor intended to signify the false surface of existence, the felled suitcases embodying the transitory nature of life—or more specifically, the life of the subject, shrimped up in the corner against a bare, mispainted wall. Naturally, it was all very funny. During another poker game at Szmura's (which I missed), everyone filed into Bogdan's chamber and found the installation uproariously amusing: they guffawed to the verge of retching and fell to the existential floor, while Bogdan sat in his corner, perplexed by all the wisecracks about his artsy-fartsiness.

He did eventually get an official tour of the apartment—an introduction to the Szmura world and its impenetrable mysteries. In the living room, with a sweeping movement of his hand, Szmura offered his furniture to Bogdan's eye: the claret velvet armchair facing a pseudo-Oriental coffee table, all Chinese curves and Japanese angles; the crimson sofa, with its wide U shape and stern, flat armrests—for some reason, Szmura referred to it as "the Puerto Rican." Bogdan was allowed to peruse the Puerto Rican when Szmura was absent, he was told; otherwise the armchair was available. Then Bogdan had to inspect the collection of objects on the mantelpiece, which consisted of an upright bullet-casing that Szmura's venerable father had brought back from Vietnam; a glass ashtray full of foreign coins (mainly kopecks and zloty); a bottle of Grolsch beer ("Be very careful," Szmura said, " 'cause this bottle is from Florida"); and a figurine of a cow, complete with a swollen udder, that was left unmentioned. Bogdan also glanced out the window, although it looked over the same alley as did the window in his room. There was nothing to see, of course, except a garage door inching downward like a stage curtain, and a few fallen deciduous leaves slipping inside before it closed.

In the bathroom, Bogdan was shown the hooks that Szmura used to hang his upper-body (navy blue) and lower-body (azure) towels and his carmine silk robe with a fire-breathing dragon on the back—Bogdan was assigned the fourth hook. He was also told that he must make a habit of lifting the toilet seat, should he put it down for the big dookie, and that he must never shave or piss in the shower. Finally, Szmura pushed a little jar into his face, its bottom lined with yellowish mites—this was where Szmura collected the wormy stuff from his nose pores.

In the kitchen, Bogdan was warned that the mug inscribed МИКОЛА, its chipped brim adorned with a traditional Ukrainian pattern, was never to be touched. The fridge contained a bowl of intensely red vine tomatoes ("They make the blood strong"), along with Szmura's black dress shoes on a tray; a plate of rotting shrimp; and a jar of Vaseline, which Bogdan could not fail to conclude was deployed for some form of self-abuse. He and Szmura did not dwell long over the contents of the pantry. Suffice it to mention a large number of Shake 'n Bake boxes stacked on the bottom shelf, and an impressive collection of soup cans lined up in alphabetical order on the top two shelves: Shelf No. 1, from Asparagus to Minestrone; Shelf No. 2, from Mushroom to Zucchini. The soup was not for Bogdan, Szmura declared.

Were he ever to open a can, he would have to replenish the collection the very same day. Concluding the tour, Szmura flung open the door of his own bedroom, and exposed briefly a darkness into which the light cut a lambent rhomboid. Bogdan was never to enter this room, not even if invited. "Think of it," Szmura said, "as a minefield."

Szmura, however, would often freely enter Bogdan's room, opening the door violently. He would launch into monolithic monologues welcoming Bogdan to this great country, which had been built by immigrants, including Szmura's own grandparents, who'd had to work hard to pull themselves up by the bootstraps and now had a condo in Orlando—which was great because it meant that there was an opportunity for everybody in this country, even a fuck-face D.P. like Bogdan. Bogdan could tell that Szmura enjoyed these speeches; he would stroke the hair coppice on his forearms as he spoke, as if petting himself.

Szmura's manner of door-opening was closely linked to his fantasies of becoming an FBI agent: he was an intern at a law office and watched *COPS* regularly, all in preparation for the FBI entrance exam, which he would take as soon as he graduated from the University of Illinois law school. Bogdan was made privy to Szmura's FBI fantasies after he unwisely agreed to a demonstration of a submission technique. He found himself on the floor, with Szmura's knee pressing against his jugular, his elbow and shoulder about to pop. "I could kill you, if I wanted to," Szmura said matter-of-factly before he let him go.

Szmura was also a note-leaver: every morning, Bogdan

would find on the kitchen table a note in a taut, wiry handwriting that corresponded somehow to the essence of Szmura—the letter T was like his body: straight, slim, angular. The notes occasionally welcomed him again (*Feel at home*), but more often they were directives (*Wash the damn dishes*) or announcements (*Rent due Tuesday*). There were some that stretched themselves thin between nonsense and poetry (*The fireplace is not real*). When Szmura, abruptly and inexplicably, started writing them down in verse form, Bogdan began collecting them. One day, from the desert covering the ruins of Chicago, a rusty box full of faded patches of paper will be excavated, and some good archaeologist will discover the soul of a perished civilization in these abstruse verses:

> *The door is either*
> *Open or locked*
> *I like*
> *Locked*

Or:

> *Your socks are all over*
> *How many fucking feet do you have?*
> *You are not alone here, buddy*
> *Not alone*

Predictably, Bogdan often retreated to his hollow room, lying in the dark, palpating the wall, as if looking for an escape tunnel. Szmura would sometimes bring home a woman—he had an unmistakable taste for the meretricious kind—and Bogdan would listen to their coital exchanges, which always seemed rehearsed, as though they were auditioning for a porn flick: she would implore Szmura to put his big dick inside her, and he would say, Oh yeah, so that's what you want, bitch, and she would say, Yeah, gimme your big dick, and he would say, Oh yeah, so that's what you want, bitch, and so it would go, until they approached the climax, when she would squeal in frequencies peculiar to the sound of a wet finger rubbing against glass, while Szmura would embark upon a volley of *fuck*s: fuckfuckfuckfuckfuckfuckfuck fuckfuckfuckfuckfuckfuckfuckfuckfuckfuckfuckfuckfuck. He occasionally encouraged his sticky companions to knock on Bogdan's door and volunteer some secondhand erotic kindness. Only one of them actually did: wearing nothing but roller skates, a buxom part-time Wicker Park waitress purred kittenishly and scratched on his door. Unable to comprehend what was going on, frightened by the screeching of the roller skates on the floor, Bogdan didn't stir. The following morning, Szmura left a note saying, *It was a hit and run / Bo / That's all it was.*

I do not know what Bogdan made of Szmura, or how aware he was of his insanity. Perhaps he was misled (as I had been) by his occasionally human impulses: he bequeathed his Shake 'n Bake collection to the Uke church, to be distributed to newly arrived immigrants; he was known to leave a tip even if the waitress was not fuckable; and one time he left a note saying, *If a bird flies in, let her out.* Most misleading of all, I think, was the polite good-boy manner that Szmura employed when discoursing with Pany Mayska, his landlady.

The day after Bogdan moved in, Szmura took him across the hall and knocked at Pany Mayska's door, a nosegay of fragrant lilies in hand. They heard the slow shuffle of her feet, and Szmura said, "Now, be nice here. No talking out of your ass." He scowled and rescowled, raising his upper lip and distending his nostrils—a grimace that Bogdan would one day learn to recognize as threatening. Pany Mayska was puny, her face powdered and centered around a small rouged mouth, her hair sparse, exposing the white streaks of her skull. She wore a pointy bra that might have been alluring half a century before, but now served as a scaffold for her cavernous chest. Szmura greeted her in Ukrainian, kissed her on the cheek, while she grabbed his lilyless hand and did not let him withdraw it, pulling him in. Her fingers were like claws, withered and twisted. Her apartment reeked of pee and pierogi, of cleanliness and ironed bedsheets. The smell traveled quickly through Bogdan's synapses until it reached the room where his grandmother had died: Ukrainian handiwork of the same geometric pattern multiplied on the tablecloth and the cushions; obsolete church calendars scattered around; a pensive etching of the poet Taras Shevchenko, glowering over his scrubby mustache; icons of bent-neck Virgins with chunky toddlers at their bosoms.

Szmura asked after Pany Mayska's health; she said it was fine—both of them all hearty smiles. Szmura might have slapped her on the back, had it not been for her frailty. And how was Victor, her grandson? Oh, he was fine, uncovering ancient Slavic grave sites near Kharkiv. He'd be home by Christmas. And how was Oksana? Ah, she still didn't have a boyfriend. "Микола, I would have liked so much to have you as my grandson-in-law." "Пани Майска, I am too young to get married," Szmura said. At this, she sighed pensively, as if Mike Szmura were the unfulfilled love of her own youth, her vanished dream.

Bogdan sat and listened with a general grin that suggested that he was interested but not prying. Pany Mayska stood up with creaking difficulty and reached for a bowl on the immaculate counter. When she put the bowl down on the table, it was full of crescent cookies. "And who are you?" she asked, pushing the bowl toward Bogdan. He gently jerked his head to express his willingness to taste a cookie, and then he told her who he was, with fatigued detachment, as if retelling the plot of a tedious Eastern European movie.

Szmura had told him that Pany Mayska used to work as a radiologist, taking X-rays of smokers' scorched lungs and the smashed hips of adventurous seniors. She was so fucking irradiated, Szmura said, that she glowed in the dark, bones coiling in her body, everything inside her rotting splendidly. Perhaps it was due to her radioactivity that Bogdan could always sense her before she knocked at their door. He would sometimes reach the door before she had even opened hers. Through the peephole, he could see her wobble over with a plateful of pierogi. She knew that Szmura was at work during the day, but she would always ask about Микола. She never agreed to come in, but she stood at the door and made him tell her, all over again, what he had told her the first time: He was a Ukrainian from Bosnia, from a small town called Prnjavor; he used to own a photo shop; he had been forced to fight for the Serbs in the war; he had escaped with nothing but the clothes he wore; and now he worked at a Jewel supermarket, packing bags until he could find something better. After Bogdan had delivered his last line, she'd hand him the plate, covered with a flimsy serviette, and displaying the same Ukrainian pattern that dominated the rest of her habitat. Then she'd deliver her own lines in the following sequence:

a. *It was terrible what was going on in Bosnia; it reminded her of the Great Famine, when millions of Ukrainians died; she prayed that it would end soon.*

b. *Bogdan should just think about all the places where Ukrainians could be found: we were everywhere from Bosnia to the jungles of Africa.*

c. *Ukrainians were very visual people, people who liked pictures; take Disney, for example, who was one of us, a Дисни—he got his many ideas, his artistic inspirations, from Ukrainian national culture, from our love of Nature.*

As rehearsed, Bogdan would extend his face into a serious smile and tighten his stomach muscles to suppress any laughter at the idea that Donald Duck was part of his heritage, that Goofy was Ukrainian. He grew to like Pany Mayska and her cookies and pierogi; he learned to bask in the glow of her radiation.

Since she had retired, she volunteered at the Museum of Ukrainian Culture and History, a funest three-story building right across the parking lot from the Jewel where Bogdan worked. Once I saw him wandering over there in a green apron and a cap that would have been fashionable in Eastern Europe decades earlier. (I was pretty sure it was he; I hadn't met him yet, but the tired gait, more than anything else, gave him away.) Pany Mayska opened the door and waived the two-dollar entrance fee with an understanding nod. Bogdan stepped into a room suffused with a green darkness, its light dammed by heavy curtains.

She looked even smaller and more radiant in the sepulchral murk. Bogdan followed her, feigning interest, past painted wooden eggs and sallow bobbin lace, his chest reverberating with sorrow. It all made him think of the shabby armoire in his grandparents' bedroom, which he had dug through as a child in search of the creased photos from their childhood. Pany Mayska ascended the stairs to a room that told, she said, the story of our people. The room was curtainless, with dust particles floating all around as the sunlight blazed outside. She pointed at a glass case under the window: a cracked bread trough; an eagle-shaped medal coated with psoriatic rust; a letter whose cursive was melting into bluish waves. Bogdan wondered whether the letter had been brought over from the old country or never sent back there from this one. Then they walked along the walls, studying photos of ghastly, famine-wasted peasants lined up for the camera, as if for execution, and portraits of stiff black-and-white men who had come over a long time ago, their eyes bulging as their tightly knotted ties cut off their airflow. Pany Mayska stopped in front of a picture of a pin-headed man with a thick mustache and round thin-rimmed glasses—that was her husband, she said, with a quiver in her voice. And then they went downstairs, to the small kitchen, where Bogdan accepted a glass of diluted raspberry concentrate, a bagful of almost expired TV dinners that she just happened to have lying around, and a report on how she had once caught Oksana and Szmura kissing, and they were only twelve years old.

I must confess that I waited in the Jewel's parking lot, with the intention of intercepting Bogdan. It was time, I thought, for us to meet. He reminded me so much of myself, as I had been not so long before: I too had had to deal with the conundrum of the Social Security number, with the recondite rules of baseball, and the immutable laws of living with Szmura. I too had resisted the temptation to slurp Szmura's soup and had accepted bags of TV dinners and dried Twinkies from Pany Mayska. Once she had even loaned me money, which I had never paid back—which was why I avoided her now, crossing the street whenever I saw her hobbling arthritically toward me.

When Bogdan stepped out of the museum, carrying a weighty paper bag, he appeared taller, clumsily hunched forward, much like Goofy. I accosted him close to the shopping cart rack. It surprised me that he wasn't surprised. He recognized me, he said—I looked like my cousin Roman, with whom he had gone to school back in Prnjavor. I had practiced my lines. I had planned to inquire about his parents and offer him my generous help. I wanted to tell him to get the hell out of Szmura's place as soon as he could. Instead, I found myself nodding meaninglessly, like a congenitally embarrassed American, to convey that he had my support and understanding, even if I could not comprehend what he was talking about. "You will never know what you escaped," he said. "You will never know how lucky you are." He told me how he had buried his parents in their backyard. He had been conscripted into the Serb army and fought at Derventa. He had seen unspeakable things: people forced into minefields, pregnant women cut open, eyes gouged out with rusty spoons, his fellow soldiers pissing into a mass grave. All he'd been able to think of was escape, so much so that he had felt relief when his parents died—though I don't know whether he said this or I just inferred it. Jewel customers— young blond mothers, old men reeking of mothballs, drunks with paper-bagged Wild Irish Rose—were responsibly returning their carts to the rack. "It is painful to remember what I cannot forget," he said, possibly quoting from a Ukrainian song I did not know. So I made up an incontestably urgent task, expressed my eagerness to get together soon, offered unspecified help, and took off across the lot. After that, I avoided him for years.

"That museum, it creeps me out, man," Szmura said, shuddering. "Why the fuck would Bo go there?"

"I don't know," I said. "Maybe it reminds him of home. Maybe he gets cozy with the old Mayska."

"Maybe you can write a nice story about that one day," Pumpek said. "Right now, you gotta deal."

"I don't understand those people. That old fucking bitch has lived in this country for fifty fucking years, and all she talks about is our people and the famine and Disney and fucking Ukraine," Szmura said.

"Deal," Pumpek said.

"It is heartbreaking," I said. "All that sorrow."

"Yeah, sure. What it is is dick-breaking," Szmura said. "You know what the Uke anthem is? 'Ukraine Hasn't Died Yet.' Hasn't fucking died *yet!* Well, let it die, man. This is America, not a psychiatric, you know, facility."

"Deal," Pumpek said.

I dealt, to Szmura and Pumpek and the two realtor guys, who said nothing, all gambling ice and calculation. One of them kept shuffling his chips while staring straight at me, obviously (and foolishly) designating me as the sucker. The other stood up and got himself a beer. I realized they were brothers.

"I am worried about Bo," Szmura said. "I want him to start living in America, stop living in the past. Those old vampires are not good for him. And he's not even from Ukraine, he is from fucking *Basnia.* I'm gonna take him under my wing. We gotta integrate him in this society."

" 'Integrate,' " the brother with the beer said all of a sudden. "Where'd you learn such a fancy word?"

And so Szmura took Bogdan under his vulture's wing. He gave him impromptu lessons in American history: he made him admire the big balls that graced the groins of the Founding Fathers; he narrated in several installments the great epic of saving the world from the freedom-hating menace (Vietnam, Grenada, the Gulf); he encouraged him to watch television to appreciate the richness of American culture; he painted the vast canvas of capitalism in a few simple strokes: free market, free enterprise, money in the bank.

One day, he invited Bogdan to sit in on a business meeting he was going to have with an acquaintance. Perhaps Bogdan was truly excited to learn something at the Szmura Institute of Integration, but more likely it was much too complicated for him to say no. Besides, Szmura had offered to let him sleep, on weeknights, on the Puerto Rican couch.

"All I want you to do," Szmura said, "is to sit there and say nothing. If I start going after the guy, or grab him by the neck, stop me. I want you to stop me." He installed Bogdan in the Puerto Rican, put a bottle of Jack Daniel's in the center of the coffee table, and a bowl of cherry tomatoes next to it. He told Bogdan that the guy who was coming over needed a favor and that it was hard for him to say no, "'cause the guy's father is the mayor of Bolingbrook." That, of course, did not sound particularly impressive to Bogdan, but before he could ask anything, Szmura was off to the kitchen to get glasses. Light filtered through the whiskey bottle, and an ocher penumbra flickered on the table.

"Everyone knows that Bolingbrook is a mob town," Szmura yelled from the kitchen. "This guy's dad has, you know, connections, and they could be useful when I'm with the FBI."

Naturally, Bogdan was uneasy at the idea of being caught between the Mob and the FBI, but he was titillated too, as anyone would be. When the doorbell rang, he leaned back in the Puerto Rican, crossed his legs, intertwined his fingers over his stomach, and tried to relax his face so it would appear sullen and cold. Szmura walked in with a tall, skinny dude in a baseball hat, seated him in the armchair, and sat next to Bogdan, whom he introduced as his "friend and associate." Jack was poured (by Bogdan), thoughts were exchanged on certain celebrity chicks and their fake tits. The skinny dude was sweating, and Szmura was spreading his arms across the back of the Puerto Rican, his forearm touching the back of Bogdan's head. He and the skinny guy both glanced at Bogdan at the same time, as if he were a conduit for an encoded transmission.

"Tell me, Michael," Szmura finally said. "How can I help you?"

"Here's my problem," Michael said, "and I don't want you to misunderstand my position here."

Bogdan felt the intense presence of Szmura and Michael in the room; he smelled their semi-criminal arousal, and everything, everything decelerated. There was a woman, Michelle. She was a great, fantastic chick, and Michael sort of loved her. (Bogdan imagined her: tall, graceful, and pensive.) But she had been having a bit of a drug problem. It had started out in college; a little pot, some E, occasionally some hard stuff, but only on weekends and holidays, when everyone else was doing it. (Bogdan saw a dark basement thumping with degenerate music, youths slumped in the corners, the whites of their eyes webbed with blood.) Michael himself had dropped it all, due to his baseball and all, and he'd been working real hard, no booze, no drugs, just clean pussy. There had been some interest from minor-league teams, pretty serious too, the Cubs' stable team, no less, a lot of money in the offing, a lot. Michelle, though, had not quit partying. She swore she got high only on weekends, but then Michael found out from a buddy of his that she was, in fact, doing shitloads of drugs. She had been fucking her dealer too, his buddy said, so Michael confronted her. (Bogdan envisioned a soundless screaming match, tears pouring off her round cheeks.) She was sorry and shit, but she admitted that she was full-hooked on coke and owed a lot of money to her dealer, some cultural-studies creep. He had forced her to fuck him. (A close-up of a woman's hand against a hairy back.) Michael went and talked to the creep, told him to fuck off. But the multiculti motherfucker wanted his money back, he was entitled to it, he had earned it, and he had some pretty big ass-whupping friends. Michael was afraid that he might force Michelle to fuck other guys to pay him off. (A tableau of panting, unctuous bodies, limbs entangled like mating snakes.)

"I hear ya," Szmura said. "So you wanna pay him off?"

"Yeah," Michael said. He needed to clean up the mess, he needed to put his money where his dick was, otherwise it would fuck up his baseball career, and baseball was his life. Bogdan did not entirely understand all of this, but the grandeur of Michael's dilemma did not escape him.

"There's plenty pussy in the sea," Szmura said.

"I am afraid I like to swim in my own pool."

"Why don't you talk to your dad?"

"My family is not known for sensitivity," he said. "I just wanna pay the motherfucker and get my woman off his dick. I'd love to have his limbs scattered all over rural Illinois, but I gotta be realistic."

"Sure," Szmura said, and looked at Bogdan, as if telepathically consulting with him. "Twenty-five percent. Standard rate among friends. How much do you need?"

"Ten G's."

"I'll have the money for you tomorrow, and a promissory note to sign too."

"I'll sign whatever you want me to."

"Fantastic," Szmura said with a snort of approbation. He grabbed a handful of tomatoes and popped them, one by one, into his mouth.

"Don't take this personally, Michael," he said, "but I feel that it is my professional obligation to mention that I would have to take measures, you know, should you fail to make a scheduled payment. I might, for one, have to talk to your dad."

"Understandable," Michael slurred.

"And for the sake of my business image"—he glanced at

Bogdan, who beamed with voyeuristic trepidation—"I might have to punish you. Nothing big, certainly not enough to endanger your baseball career, but I'm gonna have to send Bo here to address the problem."

"Understandable," Michael said, and looked at Bogdan, who, out of discomfort, folded his hands into fists—doubtless looking to Michael as if he were getting ready to smash his face in.

"Bogdan here," Szmura said, "is from *Basnia*. There was a war there, horrible stuff. He has seen things that you and I cannot begin to imagine. They slice people up over there like fucking kielbasa. So he is a little troubled, if you get what I mean. He's a bit beyond therapy. But I'm sure he'll be able to control himself, now that he knows you."

Here Bogdan fully assumed his role: he flexed his neck; he grinned at Michael, and his left incisor sparkled with the menace of a war criminal. Then he muttered, "Yes," in a deep, Slavic voice, and grabbed a couple of tomatoes. Szmura leaned back into the Puerto Rican and spread his legs triumphantly, as if to exhibit the size of his testosterone-choked testicles.

A few days later, spring parachuted into Chicago: the air was abruptly warm and fragrant, the grass was suddenly green, as if it had been painted overnight. Bogdan started growing a mustache and dreamt of buying a camera. He established an after-work ritual that involved lounging on the Puerto Rican, reading the weather forecast (*Mild with clusters of gusty morning T-storms. Clear skies in the afternoon*), while sipping a thimbleful of Jack on the rocks. His life began to contain small, repeatable pleasures.

Szmura even took him out for drinks once, to the Rainbo Club, where they would have picked up two redheaded sisters, had it not been for Bogdan's reticence. I watched them, from the far corner, where I was partly hidden behind an excitable pinball machine. Szmura did the charming, while Bogdan stared at his almost empty glass—he avoided finishing the drink because he couldn't afford to buy a round. He didn't say a word, just kept looking up at one of the sisters (her name was Julia) and smiling sheepishly. Szmura kept buying drinks, and finally he delivered his killer pick-up line: "When you get fucked up, we can take you home." Such bold-facedness had worked for him before, but this time the sisters just stood up and left, Julia bestowing a parting glance at Bogdan, which Szmura interpreted as an invitation to a fuckfest. Bogdan spent the night taking long imaginary walks with Julia, holding her imaginary hand, but didn't, in the end, dare to imagine making love to her on the spine-twisting Puerto Rican. Dawn arrived with a fanfare of chirruping sparrows, and Bogdan passed out under the weight of what could very loosely be called happiness.

He woke up late and scratched his stomach and buttocks for a while, yawning. He sauntered over to the kitchen and poured himself a cup of the feeble coffee that Szmura had kindly prepared. Then he read the note that Szmura had left on the table. He stood up to add cream to his coffee, then read it again, and this time he understood what it meant:

I am afraid, Bo,
You gonna have to go
I need your room
Michael is bringing Michelle
Pussy protection program
Pay what you can
And leave

In Bosnia, there is a typically cruel and precise idiom that is used to describe the behavior and movement of a frightened person—such an individual is said to be acting like a beheaded fly. Here was the headless Bogdan flying to his room to take off his pajamas, then collapsing on the Puerto Rican to stare for a long time at the unreal fireplace. Finally, he made it back to his room to put on his Jewel uniform, and then he headed for the pantry, as if looking for a place to hide. There he found himself facing the soup collection, despair grinding in his bowels. He read every label carefully, examined each can—but Asparagus remained stubbornly silent, Split Pea and Spinach regarded him with hatred, and he had no choice but to put his faith in the strength of Tomato. He poured what resembled congealed blood into a pot and waited for a blistery boil to break the surface. He ravenously slurped up the potion, while reading the note again, his blue shirt sprinkled with drops of red.

Pany Mayska's radiation enveloped him before he had

even knocked at her door. When she appeared, wearing slippers with pom-poms at the end of their curled tips, as if she were an aging princess from Baghdad, he told her about Szmura's note. She pressed her hand against her chest and gasped, acknowledging the imminence of hurt and humiliation. But she believed that Микола had only done what he had to do, he meant well, and it was a very small room anyway. Bogdan wanted her dried lips against his cheek; he wanted her to hold his perspiring hand and comfort him, as his grandmother would have done, but she stood away. She offered to let him stay at the museum—there was an empty room in the back—until he figured something out. A cloudlet of boiled-dough smell wafted out of her apartment, and Bogdan had the tormented feeling that he was saying good-bye to her. She gasped understandingly again, and withdrew into the darkness of her home.

The door to Szmura's room was as heavy as cast iron, as if it led to a dungeon. Bogdan entered, fully aware that once he was inside, there would be no turning back. He saw a disheveled bed, the scree of a comforter in the center, a head crater in the pillow. A full beaker of water stood by the bed, the bubbles pressing their little faces against its glass wall. A tie stretched across the chair seat, like a severed tendon. The digital clock hysterically flashed 12:00. A book (*Chicken Soup for the Baseball Fan's Soul*) spread its wings on the floor. From under the bed, a pair of stolid twenty-pound dumbbells protruded just enough for Bogdan to stub his big toe. In the closet, suits were lined up, in a spectrum of colors from azure to navy; below the suits, Szmura's shoes stood in an impeccably slanted row, like cars in a parking lot. The underwear occupied different shelves: boxers on the top, jockeys on the bottom, undershirts in the middle, all precisely aligned in stacks.

On the wall above Szmura's desk hung a map of Florida, with an inset of the Keys. On the desk, there were piles of inscrutable papers; several scattered pencils (calling up the smell of school in Prnjavor: pencil shavings, the wet chalkboard sponge, girls' freshly washed hair); a computer monitor in which Bogdan could see a curved reflection of himself; a cookie box containing baseball cards, fluorescent condoms, a pouch of pot. In the drawer, a black ball of socks; a grotesquely orange orange; a roll of twenty-dollar bills. Bogdan unrolled it and counted the money: twenty-three hundred dollars—he took eighty, then rolled it back up. There was a holstered .38 in another drawer, loaded and heavy. He unlocked it and pointed it at the window. *Bang. Bang.* He put the barrel in his mouth: it tasted metallic bitter and sweet.

A tongue of paper was hanging out of the fax machine, "Stock Alert!" and a confirmation from South Beach Heaven, "An Escort Service You Can Trust." In the garbage can he found a drawing of a dog humping a smiley face with the inscription "Fuck Ya!" On the windowsill a rotten cactus perched over a pile of photos, almost all featuring Szmura with a multicolored cocktail in his hand, surrounded by a choir of sunny young men and women. At the bottom of the pile was a sallow photo of a boy sitting sideways on a luge, his wool-capped head deposited despondently on his knees, surrounded by flat whiteness. Bogdan recognized the soporific sadness of the boy, the feeling of being stuck outside in the cold when one wanted to be inside, at home and warm.

He was folding the photo to put it in his pocket when Szmura charged across the room, leaping over the bed, and blew Bogdan's left eye right out of the socket with his first punch.

The Bees, Part 1

THIS IS NOT REAL

Many years ago my sister and I went to see a movie with our parents. The movie was about a handsome lad on a treasure hunt in Africa, in the course of which he meets a beautiful young lady he seems to get along with. Mother passed out instantly—moving pictures regularly put her to sleep. Father snorted derisively a few times, whispering into my ear: "This is stupid." He started turning to people around him, touching them as if to make them snap out of their dreams, imploring them: "People, don't believe this! Comrades! This is not real!" The audience, deeply invested in the trials and tribulations of the hero, who was presently dangling topsy-turvy over a pit of ravenous crocodiles, did not respond well to my father's prodding. An usher came by and tried, in vain, to silence him. My sister and I pretended to be focused on the screen, while our mother was woken by the ruckus only to find herself in the middle of an embarrassment. In the end, Father stormed out furiously, dragging my sister and me, Mother apologizing to the peevish audience in our wake. We took a departing look at the screen, as distant as a sunset: the hero and the disheveled (yet fair) damsel, deep in the jungle teeming with invisible villains, riding a pair of comically trotting mules.

THE NIGHTMARE IN INSTALLMENTS

My father developed his hatred of the unreal back when he was at university. One morning in his dorm room he emerged from his slumber with a clearly remembered nightmare. He immediately described it to his two roommates, the experience still disturbingly fresh in his mind. The dream involved danger, pain, and mystery, although there was also an encounter with a woman. His roommates were transfixed listening to him, while he led them down the steep, untrodden paths of his subconscious. But a moment before the face of the woman was to be revealed and the dream resolved, my father came to.

The following night, the nightmare resumed just where it had ended—the woman was beautiful and held my father's head in her lap while he wept. Then he wandered and roamed in absurdly changing landscapes; he came across talking animals, including a dog from his childhood whom his father had killed with an ax blow to the head; there were more women, including his dead mother. Then he held a watermelon with the distorted face of someone he knew but could not recognize, and when it broke open, he found a letter addressed to him. He was just about to read it when he woke up.

My father's roommates, who skipped their morning classes to hear the new developments in his troubling dreams, were sorely disappointed not to find out what was in the letter. In their afternoon classes, recounting Father's nightmare to their fellow students, they kept speculating—

titillated by the fact that it all meant something they could not grasp—what could have been in the letter, and whether the beautiful woman would ever return.

When my father woke up the following morning, the room was full of people sitting in silence, patiently waiting, their breathing slow and deep. Many eyes stared at him, as if trying to read the denouement from his face. Whatever dream my father might have had evaporated the instant his roommates asked him what was in the letter. Father did not dare disappoint them, so he opened the letter and made up the content—there was a woman who was kept in a dark dungeon by an evil man. Thence my father spun an epic narrative, obviously influenced by the archetypal picaresque stories he had read and the horror movies he had seen at the university cinema hall. Yet, even making it up, he didn't know how to end his nightmare narrative. He reached the point of confronting the evil man, but could not think of what to say, so he insisted he had to hurry to his international relations class.

And so it went on: My father would wake up to face an audience simultaneously demanding the resolution and hating the prospect thereof. But he got entangled in all his subplots and minor narratives and kept evading the conclusion, hoping it would come to him eventually. His audiences dwindled, until one of his roommates (Raf, who was to become a manic-depressive flight controller) accused him of lying. It hurt my father, for he was an honest man, but he knew that he could not say that Raf was not right. He was trapped by his own imagination, my father; he slid down the slippery slope of unreality and could not crawl back up. That was when he learned his lesson, he said. That's when he became committed to the real.

MY LIFE

One day Father came back from work with a Super 8 camera, which he had borrowed from one of his coworkers (Božo A., who had a black belt in karate and a budding brain tumor—he died before my father could return the camera). The camera was smaller than I had imagined, possessing a kind of technological seriousness that suggested only important things could be recorded with it. He announced his desire to make a film that would not lie. When my mother asked what the movie would be about, he dismissed the question as immature. "The truth," he said. "Obviously."

Nevertheless, Father wrote the script for his film in a week, at the end of which he declared that it would be the story of his life. I was cast to play the young him, and my sister to play his sister (he didn't say which one—he had five), and my mother would be his assistant. She instantly resigned from her assistant director position, as she wanted to spend her vacation reading, but the shooting was scheduled for the middle of June 1986, when we were supposed to go to the country to visit my grandparents—we would shoot, as they say, on location.

My father refused to show us the script, uninterested in the fact that the actors normally get to see scripts: he wanted life itself to be our inspiration, for, he reminded us, this film was to be *real*. Nevertheless, during our regular inspection of his desk (my sister and I went through our parents' documents and personal things to keep apprised of their development), we found the script. I'm able to reproduce it pretty accurately, since my sister and I read it to each other a few times, with a mixture of awe and hilarity. Here it is:

MY LIFE

1. *I am born.*
2. *I walk.*
3. *I watch over cows.*
4. *I leave home to go to school.*
5. *I come back home. Everybody's happy.*
6. *I leave home to go to university.*
7. *I'm in class. I study at night.*
8. *I go out for a stroll. I see a pretty girl.*
9. *My parents meet the pretty girl.*
10. *I marry the pretty girl.*
11. *I work.*
12. *I have a son.*
13. *I'm happy.*
14. *I keep bees.*
15. *I have a daughter.*
16. *I'm happy.*
17. *I work.*
18. *We are by the seaside, then in the mountains.*
19. *We are happy.*
20. *My children kiss me.*

21. *I kiss them.*

22. *My wife kisses me.*

23. *I kiss her.*

24. *I work.*

25. *The End*

FAREWELL

The first scene we were supposed to shoot (and the only one that was ever shot) was Scene 4. The location was the slope of the hill on top of which my grandparents' house was perched. I, in the role of my father at the age of sixteen, was supposed to walk away from the camera with a bundle hanging from a stick on my shoulder, whistling a plaintive melody. I was to turn around and look past the camera, as if looking at the home I was leaving—and then I would wave, bidding farewell. My father would pan to my grandparents' house, though, strictly speaking, that house was not the home he'd left.

The first take failed because I didn't wave with enough emotion. My hand, my father said, looked like a limp plucked chicken. He needed more emotion from me—I was leaving my home never to return.

The second take was interrupted as my father decided to zoom in on a bee that just happened to land on a flower nearby.

My two aunts suddenly appeared in the third take, as my father was panning from my poignant good-bye to the house. They stood grinning, paralyzed by the lens for a moment, then casually waved at the camera.

Each time, I had to walk uphill to my starting position, so I could walk away downhill in the next take. My legs hurt, I was thirsty and hungry, and I could not help questioning my father's directorial wisdom: Why wasn't he/I taking a bus? Didn't he/I need more stuff than what could fit in a bundle? Didn't he/I need some food for the road?

During the fifth take, the camera ran out of film.

The sixth take was almost perfect: I walked away from home, my shoulders slouching with sorrow, my pace aptly hesitant, the bundle dangling poignantly from the convincingly crooked stick. I turned around, completely in character, and looked at the home and life I was about to leave for good: the house was white with a red roof; the sun was setting behind it. Tears welled up in my eyes as I waved at the loving past, before heading toward an unknowable future, my hand like a metronome counting the beats of the saddest adagio. Then I heard a bee buzzing right around the nape of my neck. My metronome hand switched to allegro as I flaunted it around my head trying to defend myself. The bee would not go away, revving furiously its little engine, and the sting was imminent. I dropped the stick and started running, first uphill, toward the camera, then downhill, until my heels were kicking my butt, my arms flailing, all semblance of rhythm abandoned. The bee pursued me relentlessly and unflinchingly, and I was more terrified by its determination than the forthcoming pain: it would not quit even as I was hollering, throwing in the air all the arms I could muster, lunging at incredible speed, a manic mass of discordant movements. And the more I ran, the farther I was from any help and comfort. It was in the moment before I tripped and tumbled head over heels that I realized the bee was entangled in my hair—the attempt to escape was meaningless. I felt the sting as I was rolling downhill, toward the bottom I would never reach. I was stopped by a thornbush, where the sting became indistinguishable from many a thorn.

Need I say that my father kept filming it all? There I am, verily flapping my arms, as if trying to take off, a clueless Icarus leaping downhill farther from the skies, while a cow watches me, masticating with a sublime absence of interest, suggesting that God and his innocent creatures would never give a flying fuck about the fall of man. Then I tumble and hit the bush of thorns, and my father, with a cold presence of his directorial mind, my father fades me out.

OTHER WORKS

To my father's creative biography I should add his carpentry, which frequently reached poetic heights: more than once we witnessed him caressing or kissing a piece of wood he was about to transform into a shelf, a stool, or a beehive frame; not infrequently, he forced me to touch and then smell a "perfect" piece of wood; he demanded that I appreciate the smooth knotlessness, its natural scent. For Father, a perfect world consisted of objects you could hold in your hand.

He built all kinds of things: structures to hold my mother's plants, toolboxes, beds and chairs, beehives, et cetera, but his carpenterial masterpiece was a nailless kitchen table he spent a month building. He paid a price: one afternoon he emerged from his workshop, his palm sliced open with a chisel, the blood gushing and bubbling from its center, as from a well—a detail worthy of a biblical miracle. He drove himself to the hospital, and afterward the car looked like a crime scene.

He also liked to sing anything that allowed his unsophisticated baritone to convey elaborate emotional upheavals. I remember the evening I found him sitting in front of the TV, with a notebook and an impeccably sharpened pencil, waiting for the musical show that was sure to feature his favorite song at the time: "Kani Suzo, Izdajice"—"Drop, You Traitor Tear." He wrote down the words, and in the days that followed he sang "Kani Suzo, Izdajice" from the depths of his throat, humming through the lyrics he couldn't recall, getting ready for future performances. He sang at parties and family gatherings, sometimes grabbing a mistuned guitar from someone's hand, providing accompaniment that comprised the same three chords (Am, C, D7) regardless of the song. He seemed to believe that even a severely mistuned guitar provided "atmosphere," while the harmonic simplification enhanced the emotional impact of any given song. There was something to be said for that: it was hard to deny the power of his baritone against the background of the discordant noise worthy of Sonic Youth, a tear glimmering in the corner of his eye, on the verge of committing betrayal.

His photography merits a mention, even if its main function was to record the merciless passing of time. Most of his photos are structurally identical despite the change of clothes and background: my mother, my sister, and I facing the camera, the flow of time measured by the increasing amounts of my mother's wrinkles and gray hair, the width of my sister's beaming smile, and the thickness of the smirking and squinting on my face.

One more thing: He once bought a notebook, and on the first page wrote: *This notebook is for expressing the deepest thoughts and feelings of the members of our family.* It seemed he intended to use those feelings and thoughts as material for a future book, but few were expressed. I, for one, certainly wasn't going to let my parents or my sister (ever eager to tease me to tears) in on the tumultuous events in my adolescent soul. Thus there were only two entries: a cryptic note from my mother, who probably just grabbed the notebook while on the phone and wrote:

Friday
Healthy children
Thyme

and a line from my sister, in her careful and precise prepubescent handwriting:

I am really sad, because the summer is almost over.

Whatever conveyed reality earned my father's unqualified appreciation. He was suspicious of broadcast news, relentlessly listing the daily triumphs of socialism, but was addicted to the weather forecast. He read the papers, but found only the obituaries trustworthy. He loved nature shows, because the existence and the meaning of nature were self-evident—there was no denying a python swallowing a rat, or a cheetah leaping on the back of an exhausted, terrified monkey.

My father, I say, was deeply and personally offended by anything he deemed unreal. And nothing insulted him more than literature; the whole concept was a scam. Not only that words—whose reality is precarious at best—were what it was all made from, but those words were used to render *what never happened*. This dislike of literature and its spurious nature may have been worsened by my intense interest in books (for which he blamed my mother) and my consequent attempts to get him interested. For his forty-fifth birthday I unwisely gave him a book called *The Liar*—he read nothing of it but the title. Once I read him a passage from a García Márquez story in which an angel falls from the skies and ends up in a chicken coop. After this my father was seriously concerned about my mental capacities. There were other, similar incidents, all of them appalling enough for him to start casually mentioning his plan to write a *real* book.

He didn't seem to think that writing such a book was a

particularly trying task—all one needed to do was not get carried away by indulgent fantasies, stick to what really happened, hold on to its unquestionable firmness. He could do that, no problem; the only thing he needed was a few weeks off. But he could never find a time: there was his job, and bees, and things to be built, and the necessary replenishing naps. Only once did he approach writing anything—one afternoon I found him snoring on the couch with his notebook on his chest and a pencil with a broken tip on the floor, the only words written: *Many years ago.*

THE WRITER'S RETREAT

My father began writing in Canada, in the winter of 1994. They had just landed, after a couple of years of exile and refugee roaming, the years I spent working low-wage jobs and pursuing a green card in Chicago. They had left Sarajevo the day the siege began and went to my deceased grandparents' house in the countryside, ostensibly to escape the trouble. The real reason was that it was time for the spring works in my father's apiary, which he kept at the family estate. They spent a year there, on a hill called Vučijak, living off the food they grew in the garden, watching trucks of Serbian soldiers going to the front. My father occasionally sold them honey, and toward the end of that summer started selling mead, although the soldiers much preferred getting drunk on slivovitz. My parents secretly listened to the radio broadcast from the besieged Sarajevo and feared a knock at the door in the middle of the night. Then my mother had a gallbladder infection and nearly died, so they went to Novi Sad, where my sister was attempting to complete her university degree. They applied for a Canadian immigration visa, got it, and arrived in Hamilton, Ontario, in December 1993.

From the window of the fifteenth-floor unfurnished apartment they moved into they could see piles of snow, the smokestacks of the Hamilton steel mills, and a vacant parking lot. It was all black and white and bleak and gray, like an existentialist European movie (which my father found unreal without exception, and morbidly boring on top of it). He started despairing as soon as he set foot on Canadian soil: he didn't know where they had landed, how they were going to live and pay for food and furniture; he didn't know what would happen to them if one of them got terribly sick. And it was perfectly clear to him that he would never learn the English language.

My mother, on the other hand, let her stoic self take over—partly to counterbalance my father's darkest fears, partly because she felt so defeated that it didn't matter anymore. It was okay now to give herself to the tragic flow of things and let happen whatever was going to happen. My mind stores an image of her patiently and unfalteringly turning a Rubik's Cube in her hands, while a report on a Sarajevo massacre is on TV, completely unfazed by the fact that she is not, and never would be, anywhere close to the solution.

Soon enough, my mother set up the apartment with the used furniture her English teacher had given them. The place still looked hollow, devoid of all those crumbles of a lived life that lead you back home: the heavy green malachite ashtray Father brought back from Zaire; a picture of me and my sister as kids, sitting in a cherry tree, smiling, my sister's cheek pressing against my arm, me holding on to a branch with both of my hands like a chimpanzee (I fell off the tree and broke my arm the instant after the picture was taken); a spider brooch my mother kept in a heavy crystal ashtray; a moisture stain on a bathroom pipe that looked like an unshaven, long-haired Lenin; honey jars with labels that had little bees flying out of the corners toward the center, where the words "Real Honey" stood out in boldface—none of those things was there, now slowly fading into mere memories.

My father dropped out of his English class, furious at the language that randomly distributed meaningless articles and insisted on having a subject in every stupid sentence. He made cold calls to Canadian companies and in unintelligible English described his life, which included being a diplomat in the world's greatest cities, to perplexed receptionists who would simply put him on indefinite hold. He nearly got sucked into a venture set up by a shady Ukrainian who convinced him there was money in smuggling Ukrainian goose down and selling it to the Canadian bedding industry.

Sometimes I'd call from Chicago and my father would pick up the phone.

"So what are you doing?" I'd ask.

"Waiting," he'd say.

"For what?"

"Waiting to die."

"Let me talk to Mom."

And then, one day, when his woe became so overwhelming that his soul physically hurt, like a stubbed toe or a swollen testicle, he decided to write. He wouldn't show his writing to my mother or sister, but they knew he was writing about bees. Indeed, one day in the early spring of 1994, I received a manila envelope with another envelope inside, on which was written, in a dramatic cursive, *The Bees, Part 1.* I have to confess that my hands trembled as I flipped through it, as if I were unrolling a sacred scroll, uncovered after a thousand years of sleep. The sense of sanctity, however, was diminished by a huge, sticky honey stain on page six.

THE BEES, PART I

There is something faithfully connecting our family and bees, my father starts his narrative. *Like a member of the family, the bees have always come back.*

He then proudly informs the reader that it was his grandfather Teodor (the reader's great-grandfather) who brought civilized beekeeping to Bosnia, where the natives still kept bees in straw-and-mud hives and killed them with sulfur, *all of them,* to get the honey. He remembers seeing straw-and-mud hives in the neighbors' backyards, and they looked strange to him, a relic from the dark ages of beekeeping. He recounts the story of the few hives that arrived with the family from the hinterlands of Ukraine to the promised land of Bosnia—the only thing promised was plenty of wood, which enabled them to survive the winters. The few hives multiplied quickly, the development of beekeeping in northwestern Bosnia unimpeded by World War One. My grandfather Ivan, who was twelve when he arrived in Bosnia (in 1912), became the first president of the Beekeeping Society in Prnjavor. My father describes a photograph of the Society's founding picnic: Grandfather Ivan stands in the center of a large group of nicely dressed peasants with a then fashionable long mustache and dandily cocked hat. Some of the peasants proudly exhibit faces swollen with bee stings.

Sometimes there were interesting mischiefs with bees, my father writes, failing to mention any *mischiefs.* The sudden sentence is one of his many stylistic idiosyncrasies: his voice wavers from establishment of the historical context with a weighty, ominous phrase like *War was looming across that dirt road* or *Gods of destruction pointed their irate fingers at our honey jars* to the highly technical explanations of the revolutionary architecture of his father's hives; from the discussion of the fact that bees die a horrible death when they sting (and the philosophical implications thereof) to the poetical descriptions of hawthorn in bloom and the piping of the queen bee the night before the swarm is to leave the hive.

Father devotes nearly a page to the moment he first recognized a queen bee. *A hive contains about 50,000 bees,* he writes, *and only one queen.* She's noticeably bigger than other bees, who dance around her, swirl and move in *peculiar, perhaps even worshipful ways.* His father pointed at the queen bee on a frame heavy with bees and honey, and, my father writes, *it was like reaching the center of the universe*—the vastness and the beauty of the world were revealed to him, *the logic behind it all.*

In an abrupt transition, he asserts that *the most successful period of our beekeeping ended in 1942, during World War Two, when we for the first time lost our bees.* It is clear that was a major catastrophe for the family, but my father keeps everything in perspective, probably because of what was going on in the besieged Sarajevo at the time of his writing. *There are worse things that can happen to you. A whole family, for example, can perish without a trace,* he writes. *We didn't perish, which is excellent.*

He then draws a little map at the center of which is the hill of Vučijak, near the town of Prnjavor, whose name appears at the fringe of the page. He draws a straight line from Prnjavor to Vučijak (*6 kilometers,* he writes along the line), ignoring the creeks, the forests, and the hills in between (including the hill I tumbled down). He places little stars around the page, which seem to represent different villages and people in that area. *It was a truly multinational place,* he says, wistfully. *Germans, Hungarians, Czechs, Poles, Ukrainians, Slovaks, Italians, Serbs, Muslims, Croats, and all the mixed ones.* He calculates that there were seventeen different nationalities—there was even a tailor in Prnjavor who was Japanese. Nobody knew how he got there, but when he died, there were only sixteen nationalities left. (Now, I have to say that I've inquired about the Japanese tailor, and no one else remembers him or has heard about him.) In 1942, lawlessness was rampant, and there were roaming gangs of Serbs and Croatian fascists and Tito's partisans too. All those *others*, who had no units of their own, save the Germans, were suspect and vulnerable. One day, two *semi-soldiers* showed up at the door of the family's house. They were their neighbors, ordinary peasants, except for their rickety rifles and caps with the partisan red star in the front and the Chetnik insignia (an ugly eagle spreading its mighty wings) in the back—they switched according to need. There was going to be a great battle, the peasants said, the mother of all battles. *They said we should be well advised to leave.* The peasants said they would padlock everything, and *they showed us a huge key, for which obviously no padlock existed.* They suggested, touching the knives at their belts as if inadvertently, that *we take only what we could carry. Father begged them to let us take a cow; my mother, five sisters, and two brothers wept. Winter was around the corner.* Perhaps it was the weeping that made these neighbors take pity and let my father's family bring a cow, although it was the sick one—her shrunken udder would not provide any milk or solace. *And we left thirty beehives behind.*

My father's handwriting changes at the beginning of the next paragraph; the thick letters thin out; his cursive becomes unstable; there are a couple of crossed-out sentences. Under the shroud of fierce scratching I can make out several words and discontinuous phrases: *urine . . . aspirin . . . belonging to . . . and skin . . . scythe.*

I was six years old, he continues after the interruption, *and I was carrying a meat grinder.* His mother was carrying his youngest brother—*he hung to her chest like a little monkey.* His brother was sobbing and clutching a picture of two children crossing a bridge over troubled water, *a chubby angel hovering over them.*

Only after a few months did *all the details of the pillaging and pilfering done by the neighbors* come to light, but my father doesn't list the details. After they had emptied the house and the attic and the barn, they finally got to the bees. All they wanted was honey, even if there was not much, just enough to help the bees survive the winter. They opened the hives and shook the bees off the frames. The bees were helpless: this was late October, it was cold, and they couldn't fly or sting. They dropped to the ground in absolute silence: *no buzz, no life; they all died that night.* When the family returned home, my father saw a mushy pile of rotting bees. *Before they died, they crawled closer together to keep warm.*

A few hives were stolen by Tedo, a neighbor, who also was a beekeeper. Grandfather Ivan knew that Tedo had some of our bees, but he never asked for them. Tedo came by one day and, unable to look Grandfather Ivan in the eye, claimed that he was only taking care of the bees while the family was away. He offered to give them back. *I remember going with my father to retrieve our hives. We went on a sleigh and we had to be careful not to shake our two hives, lest the bees unfurl their winter coils, which kept them warm.* My father sat between the hives, holding them, on their way back. It was a cold night, *with stars glittering like ice shards.* If they were careful and patient, his father told him, these two hives would breed many more. The following year they had six hives, and then twice as many, and in a few years they had twenty-five.

THE CONDITIONS OF PRODUCTION

I ought to respect my father's desire—indeed, his need—to produce a real book. Hence I must spend a few paragraphs on the conditions of his truth production. Of course, I wasn't there at the time, so I have to use the accounts of reliable witnesses (my mother, mainly). Thus: He wrote mainly in the afternoon, with a pencil, on filler paper, in a diplomat's slanted cursive. He sharpened his pencil with a Swiss Army knife (his duty-free present to himself from years before), littering the bedroom floor with shavings, sitting on the bed with the nightstand between his legs. The pencils, bought in a dollar store, broke their tips frequently, and he snapped them, infuriated. Over the phone, I had to listen to elaborate laments and retroactive appreciation of "our" pencils, which would last and which you could trust. Sometimes he'd just sit there staring at the smokestacks of Hamilton or hissing at the pigeons on the balcony, attracted by the bread crumbs my mother had left for them. He'd often interrupt his inspiration-gathering time by getting himself a slice of bread with butter and honey. Eventually he would start writing, and would sometimes keep at it for as long as forty-five minutes—an eternity for someone who had a heart rate perpetually above normal, someone as impatient and miserable as my father.

I'm holding his manuscript in my hand right now, and I can see the ebb and flow of his concentration; I can decode his back pain increasing and decreasing: smooth, steady handwriting at the top of, say, page ten, which then meanders on page eleven; random words written in the margins (*dwarf . . . horsemen . . . watermelon . . . slaughter*); complete sentences pierced by the straight lance of the writer's discontent (*Beekeeping was an attractive summer activity*); adjectives keeping company with lonely, arid nouns (*stinky* wafting around *feet*; *classic* accompanying *theft*; *golden* melting over *honey*). Toward page thirteen, one can sense longer breaks between sentences, the thickly penciled words thinning out after a sharpening session. There are mid-sentence breaks, with syntactical discrepancies between independent and dependent clauses, suggesting his thought splitting, the splinters flying off in different directions. Sometimes the sentence simply ceases: *We know*, then nothing; *It must be said*, but it is impossible to know what must be said.

And something troubling and strange happens around page seventeen. My father is in the middle of conveying a humorous story about Branko, a neighbor, yet again a victim of a bee attack. At this point in the narrative, Grandfather Ivan is in charge of a socialist-collective apiary, because all his hives have been taken away by the co-op. He is in charge of about two hundred hives—far too many to keep in one place, *but an order is an order.* My father, thirteen at the time, is helping him. *The day is gorgeous; the birds are atwitter; there is an apple tree in the center of the apiary, its branches breaking with fruit.* They work in complete, profound silence, interrupted only by the occasional thud of a ripe apple falling to the ground. A swarm of bees is hanging from one of the branches, and they need to get the bees into a hive. Grandpa Ivan will shake the branch, while my father holds the hive under it, and when the swarm hits the hive, it'll just settle in, following the queen. *But I might be too weak to hold the hive, and if the swarm misses it, they might just fall on me. Now, they don't sting when they're swarming, but if they fall down with their stings first, they might still hurt me. What's more, we would have to wait for them to gather again. My father is contemplating the situation.* Here comes Branko, clearly up to no good. He hates bees, because he's been stung so many times, but he offers his help. He probably hopes he'll be able to steal something, or spy on Grandpa Ivan, who accepts his help. So Branko stands under the swarm, fretfully looking up at the bees, trotting around in a small circle, trying to center the hive. As he's still moving, Grandpa Ivan shakes the branch with a long, crooked stick, and the swarm falls directly on Branko. Before a single sting breaks his skin, Branko is screaming and shaking his head and shoulders and sides as if possessed by a host of demons.

The paragraph breaks off as Branko stampedes out of the apiary, then crashes through a hedge and throws himself into a mud puddle, while a humongous sow, the mud-puddle proprietress, looks at him, lethargically perplexed. My father is rolling on the ground with laughter, while a twitch that could be a smile surfaces on Grandpa Ivan's face, then quickly vanishes.

In the next paragraph, in cursive so tense and weak that it seems evanescent, my father talks about an epidemic that attacked the co-op hives, rapidly spreading, as they were much too bunched up, and decimating the bee population. He describes the harrowing image of *a thick layer of dead bees glimmering in the grass.* Grandpa Ivan is squatting despondently, leaning on a tree, surrounded by rotting apples that beckon hysterical flies. *This is life,* my father concludes, *struggle after struggle, loss after loss, endless torment.*

FATHERS AND DAUGHTERS

It took me a while to find out what had happened between the paragraphs. My source confirmed that the break was one month long, at the beginning of which time my father received a call from Nada, his first cousin Slavko's daughter, who had emigrated, alone, from Vrbas, Yugoslavia, and ended up in Lincoln, Nebraska. She had gone to college there, majoring in library science and minoring in theology. Slavko grew up with my father—they were the same age—and had recently died as an accomplished alcoholic. Nada called my father, because, she said, her father had told her childhood stories: the games, the adventures, the poverty—their childhood, he'd said, was golden. My father was delighted, told her to call anytime, for "family is family." There followed a few phone calls, but they were too expensive, for both Nada and my father, so they started exchanging letters. Instead of writing *The Bees,* my father reminisced in letters to Nada, fondly recalling his and Slavko's childhood *mis-chiefs,* implicitly listing his losses. My mother said that if Nada hadn't been his family and thirty or so years younger, she would've thought that my father was in love. There was now someone he could paint his life for, practically from the first scratch, someone to whom he could tell the true story.

I've never seen Nada's letters, but my mother says they were often ranting, bemoaning the fact that, despite the golden childhood, her father ended up a weak, bitter man. And her mother was overly receptive to the attention of other men. And her brother was not very smart and she never had anything in common with him. She also hated America and Americans, their provincialism, their stupid, rootless culture of cheeseburgers and cheap entertainment. She was clearly wretched, my mother said, but my father was by and large oblivious of that. His letters were rife with apples of indescribable taste (unlike the apples you got in Canada, which tasted as if they had been dry-cleaned) and family get-togethers where everybody sang and hugged and licked honey from the tips of their fingers.

Then, after a break in correspondence and many unreturned messages my father left on her voicemail, Nada faxed an unfinished sixty-five-page letter in the middle of the night—my parents were woken by an avalanche of paper slithering out of their fax machine. In the fax, her father was upgraded to a child molester, her mother to a cheap prostitute, her brother to a compulsive, shameless masturbator. America had evolved into a filthy inferno of idiocy and nothingness run by the Jews and the CIA. Her roommate (a Latina whore) was trying to kill her; her professors discussed her with her classmates when she was not around, showing secretly taken pictures of her naked body, before which frat boys frantically masturbated. Her physician tried to rape her; they refused to sell her milk in the supermarket; in the INS office, where she went to apply for her green card, the woman who interviewed her was touching herself under the desk and had hooves instead of feet; and somebody was changing the words in the books she was studying from—every day, the books were full of new *lies, lies, lies.* She had first believed that she was persecuted by jealous people, who hated her because she was virginally pure, but now she believed that God had become evil and begun purging the innocent. *The only hope I have is you,* she wrote on page sixty. *Could you come and take me from this pit of hell?* Then, in the last few pages, before the fax abruptly ended, she warned my father about me, reminded him of the Oedipus myth and the fact that I lived in the United States, which meant that I was corrupt and untrustworthy. *Keep in mind,* she wrote, *that God preferred sons to fathers and daughters.*

I had never met Nada or her father. At the peril of being maudlin, or appearing malicious, let me note that her name translates as "hope." I have since seen this fax from hell: its hysterical letters and exclamation points are faded, because of fax toner shortage and the passing of time.

A DIFFERENT STORY

My father kept calling Nada, receiving no answer, until her meretricious roommate, one Madrigal, picked up the phone and told my father that Nada had been "institutionalized." He did not understand the word, and could not pronounce it for me to translate it, so I called Madrigal. "She just went nuts," Madrigal told me. "In the library. She heard voices coming from the books, spreading hateful rumors about her."

My father was devastated. He called someone at the University of Nebraska and in his Tarzan English asked this person to visit Nada at the institution and tell her that he had called. "We don't do that," the anonymous Nebraskan said. Father sat at his nightstand, frantically sharpening his pencil, but not writing, until it was reduced to a stump he could barely hold between his fingers. He called every member of the family he could reach, as if they could pool their mental waves and send a telepathic remedy to Nada. He called me almost every day and then demanded that I immediately call him back, as they could not afford those calls. He gave me reports of his futile attempts to reach Nada, and finally asked me to go to Lincoln and track her down, but I couldn't do it. "You've become American," he said disconsolately. But that's a different story.

THE MESSAGE

After the break, his story trickles away with unmentioned sorrow. My father flies through an incident in which Grandpa Ivan was stung by hundreds of bees, and consequently spent a few days in what by all accounts must have been a coma. *But he never again felt the back pain that had tortured him for years.*

He devotes a paragraph to beekeeping in the sixties and seventies, *which could be considered the second golden age of*

family beekeeping, even if Father was going completely blind.
When Grandpa Ivan eventually lost his sight, the bees slowly
died off, and shortly before his death there were only three
hives left. My father couldn't help with the beekeeping.
*Traveling and working around the world, mainly in the Middle
East and Africa, I could barely manage to see my parents three
times a year, and there was no way I could devote any of my time
to the bees.*

There is a presence of regret in the space between the
previous sentence and the next (and last) one:

*Shortly before his death, Father summoned me and my broth-
ers for a meeting on the family beekeeping tradition. His message*

And there *The Bees, Part 1* ends, no message ever delivered, though it is easy to imagine what it might have been.
My grandfather died, my grandmother too, my father, along
with his brothers, kept the bees. They (the bees) survived a
varroa epidemic, a drought, and the beginning of the war in
Bosnia. When the family emigrated to Canada, they left behind twenty-five hives. Shortly after their departure, a horde
of their neighbors, all drunken volunteers in the Serbian
army, came at night and kicked the hives off their stands,
and when the bees feebly tried to escape (it was night, cold
again, they crept on the ground), the neighbors threw a couple of hand grenades and laughed at the dead bees flying
around as though alive. The neighbors then stole the heavy
frames, and left a trail of dripping honey in their wake.

THE WELL

My father found a job in a Hamilton steel mill, filling wagons with scrap metal. The mill was hot in the summer, cold in the winter, and when he worked night shifts, he would sometimes fall asleep waiting for a green light at the wheel of a used, decrepit Lincoln Town Car. He'd say that his Lincoln brought him home while he was sleeping, like a faithful horse. He hated the job, but had no choice.

One day, surveying the ads in the papers, pursuing a perfect garage sale, he found an ad selling honey. He called the number and told the man outright that he had no money to buy the honey, but that he would love to see his bees. Because there is such a thing as beekeepers' solidarity, the man invited him over. He was a Hungarian, a retired carpenter. He let my father help him with the bees, gave him old copies of *Canadian Beekeeping*, which my father tried to read with insufficient help from my mother's dictionary. After a while, the Hungarian gave him a swarm and an old hive to start his own apiary. He admonished my father for refusing to wear beekeeping overalls and hat, even gloves, but my father contended that stings were good for all kinds of pain. I still can't figure out what language they might have been speaking to each other, but it almost certainly wasn't English.

My father has twenty-three beehives now and collects a few hundred pounds of honey a year, which he cannot sell. "Canadians don't appreciate honey," he says. "They don't understand it." He wants me to help him expand into the

American market, but I assure him that Americans understand honey even less than Canadians do.

He has recently decided to write another true book. He already has the title: *The Well.* There was a well near their home when he was a boy. Everybody went there to get water. *The Well* would be a story about people from the village and their cattle, their intersecting destinies. Sometimes there were "interesting incidents." Once, he remembers, somebody's mule escaped and came to the well, sensing water. But its head was tied to its leg—that's how people forced the mules to graze. The mule got away, found water, but then was unable to drink. It lingered around the well, furiously banging its head against the trough, dying of thirst, the water inches away. And it brayed, in horrible pain. *It brayed all day,* my father says. *All day and all of the night.*

Whe n I was in grammar school, I most loved the weeks when I was the *redar*, the one in charge of cleaning the chalkboard. My job was to keep the sponge wet and to wipe the chalkboard when the teacher demanded it. I took pleasure in erasing everything, in the smell of moistened chalk and the dryness of my hands afterward, and I loved leaving the classroom to wash the sponge in the bathroom. The hallway would be silent and empty, redolent of clean children and floor wax. I relished the squeaking of my shoes, the echoes in the void; I walked to the bathroom slowly, adjusting my steps to produce a screechy rhythm. There was something exhilarating about being free and alone in that vacant space while the rest of the kids were interned in the classrooms, to be released only at the break. I would wash the sponge without urgency, then walk back extending every step to delay my return to class. Now and then, I would stop by the door of a classroom and eavesdrop on what was going on inside. I would hear the murmur of the compliant children and the steady, solemn voice of the teacher. What gladdened me was that nobody knew I was out there unbound, listening. They could not see me, but I could hear everything; they were inside, and I was outside.

"Why was that so exciting?" Alma asked, and looked at

the little digital camera screen, as though to check whether I was still there.

"I don't know. I felt free," I said. "There, but not there."

She'd said she was a great admirer of my work and, as a fellow Bosnian, she'd felt that in my books I was speaking directly to her. She'd spoken directly to me via my website and at first I ignored her message, but then she sent me another one threatening with her disappointment. Ever reluctant to disappoint people, I responded. Her name was Alma B.; she was a film student at NYU and a Bosnian, therefore interested in questions of "identity"; she wanted to make films about "the Bosnian experience." Which brought her to the real reason for contacting me: for her final project, she wanted to make a film about me, to tell the story of my life and displacement, the loss and the transformation, my complicated identifications.

All of my identities are at your disposal, I cleverly wrote back.

We went on corresponding, and she asked me many thorny questions. It usually took me days to answer them, in long, repetitive e-mails, rambling about anything that came to my mind: my family history and the war crimes of the Bush regime; my thoughts on rock 'n' roll and quantum physics; my theory of soccer and poetry; the epistemology of Conrad and Rimbaud and myself. I told her the stories of my life, embellishing here, flatly making things up there, for I frankly wanted to help her write a good script and get the funding for her project. I even meekly nudged her toward a short film in which I could play myself in various situations from my life—one of those brainy postmodern setups everybody likes so well because it has something to do with identity—but she gently rejected the idea. I flirted with her too, for, as everybody knows, the job of the writer is to seduce his readers. For some reason I kept all of our exchanges.

When her project proposal was finally approved, I suggested that she fly to Chicago to meet me, but she thought she ought to start from the beginning, find out more about me and talk to my parents first. So she drove up to Hamilton, Ontario, on a weekend. My parents took her to be a friend of mine and therefore another one of their children; on arrival she had to promise that she would stay overnight. Mother dug deep into her repertoire of cakes and pies, for she knew you could not fool a real Bosnian with bad Canadian food; Father summoned our kin, including a cousin with an accordion, to sing a selection of songs and drink to her health and the health of her family, then to her health again. And she videotaped the whole thing: their drunken singing, my father telling her about the film he had once directed, my mother telling her about my troubled adolescence—it must have been a catastrophe, I thought when I heard about it. It was not hard to imagine my intoxicated family seriously undermining the image of the noble, worldly misfit who found his salvation in writing, the image I had so carefully and publicly established. They told Alma everything, things I was amazed they could recall at all: they told her about the time I had been caught stealing hubcaps; about our young, pretty neighbor taking me by the ear to my parents so I could admit I had leapt at her from the darkness and grabbed one of her rather large breasts; about my suffering from a crew of bullies, whose meanness eventually compelled one of my classmates (Predrag was his name, I believe) to blow his brains out. And to me it wasn't even about the damage to my image, it was that if those stories should have ever been told, I was the only one who was supposed to do that—I was the only professional storyteller in the family.

I tried to find out from my parents how Alma had reacted to their divulgations—for I did not want to disappoint her before I even met her—but they assured me there was nothing to worry about. Even when telling potentially compromising stories they rendered me lovingly and likably; my parents were (and still are) conventional and reasonable, always willing to dismiss any kind of alarmingly refractory behavior as "a phase." And they did also convey their warm memories of our quaint summer vacations by the sea, and how they had let me swim in the deep waters, confident that I would come back to the shallows the moment I heard their whistle. (I remember the damn whistle: black, smelling of spit, with a baffling chickpea inside.) Alma later showed me the footage of them tearing up while recollecting our winter vacations, our mountain cabin, to which I went alone in the summer, they told her, to devour fat books and write stories and poems.

My parents liked Alma quite a bit. She was a true Bosnian girl, they thought: respectful of the elderly, kindhearted and polite, still unspoiled by America. "She can talk to anybody and everybody," my mother said. "She doesn't think she's special." They practically offered to adopt her; indeed, ever worried about my procreation, they suggested not so abashedly that we could be a good match. When I called them after Alma's visit, they both got on the phone to laud her.

"She came to America alone. She had an aunt in New York," my mother said. "She was only thirteen when she arrived. She is very smart."

"Where you throw her, there she lands," my father said. "But she didn't have an aunt in New York, she had an older brother. And she was sixteen when she arrived."

"No, no, she said her brother was killed by a sniper in Sarajevo. And her father had a heart attack in the war, and her mother died of cancer right after the war," my mother said, and sighed. "Your father never pays any attention."

"I pay attention," my father said, irritated. "Her mother was killed by a sniper, and her father died after the war."

"Listen to him. He never listens to me, or anybody else. That's what I've had to deal with my whole life: I send him to buy detergent, he comes back with three cartons of milk, and we already have a fridge full of milk. What am I to do with all that milk?" my mother said. "I wish I had been shot by a sniper."

Naturally, when Alma came to Chicago to interview me, I didn't dare ask her to sort out who in her family died of cancer and who was shot by a sniper. But she evinced the

kind of serenity earned through suffering, therefore un-
attainable by—perhaps even invisible to—those who had not
experienced severe loss and pain; I understood why my parents liked her. I watched her as she was mounting her digital
camera on a tripod in my office: the short, ascetic hair and
the deft, determined hands; the large, heart-shaped head
dominated by grand, dramatically dark eyes; the delicate
frown of focus. Her body bespoke a hardened core, an irreversibly petrified toughness, the scar tissue of the soul, but I
could still see the little Alma in her, the way she used to be as
a grammar school girl: wearing a white shirt and a blue skirt,
white stockings and red shoes, her long hair shimmering,
meticulously combed by her mother. "Okay, let's go," she
said when she was ready, and I had no choice but to begin.

I introduced myself to the camera, told it where I was
born, described the part of Sarajevo by the old train station
where I grew up. I am so old, I said by way of a joke, I can
remember steam trains. We used to crawl under the trains
resting in the station, then pull a plug and let the steam out;
I burned my shins that way at least once. There was also a
movie theater nearby, Kino Arena, and we would go to the
movies all the time. My childhood was wonderfully socialist
and there was no movie-rating shit, so we could watch whatever we wanted: spaghetti westerns, kung fu movies, German soft porn, communist war epics, all kinds of American
trash—I grew up on a steady diet of sex and violence, I said,
and there is absolutely nothing wrong with me, is there?

Abruptly and indelicately, she asked me about the phase
when I had impersonated an American commando, pretend-

ing to be speaking English all the time. My parents told her that I had had a rifle I would not part with; they had described how I had imagined and executed combat operations in my room, sometimes in the middle of the night, waking my little sister, who would in turn wake them with her screams.

"Do you remember that?" she asked. "Can you tell me a little bit about you imagining yourself as an American?"

Amazed once again that my parents could remember that particular phase, I could not fathom the point of recollecting that story. One builds one's life on consistency; one invests it with the belief, however unsupported by reality, that one has always been what one is now, that even in one's distant past one could recognize the seed from which this doomed flower has bloomed. Now I could not understand the devout thoroughness of my childhood obsessions, the myriad origins of my overactive imagination—I could not quite summon who I used to be. The camera, I am sure, duly recorded my fidgeting, the shadow passing over my face, the titillating doubt and vulnerability. But once you get in front of the inquiring lens, it is hard to look away; once you start inventing and soliloquizing, it is terribly hard to quit.

Yes, when I was ten or so, I wanted to be an American commando, I admitted, but you have to understand the larger context.

I spent most of my childhood fighting various wars. An early one was inspired by the TV series *Quentin Dedward*: we divided ourselves in two groups and had sword fights with sticks. Since young Quentin was fighting his enemies over a fair damsel, and we had no interest in girls as such, let alone fair damsels, it was over in a week, as soon as our sticks started breaking. Then there was an ongoing war in which we were the partisans fighting the Germans. This one was, of course, inspired by the narrative and the films of the Yugoslav liberation as accomplished by Tito and our heroic people. For the Liberation War, we used the sticks as guns. We set up ambushes in the bushes; we threw rocks as hand grenades in suicidal charges at German bunkers; we attacked the innocently passing streetcars, which were in fact enemy convoys delivering the necessary fuel and supplies to the desperate Army Group D. The trouble with this war was that we didn't have a real enemy: none of us wanted to be a German, because nobody ever wanted to be evil. We shot at nobody, we threw rocks into thin air, the streetcar attacks were too risky to do too often, particularly since a conductor caught my friend Vampir and slapped him bloody. War is an entirely different thing when you can't enjoy your wicked enemy's dying a horrible, prolonged, painful death.

Then there was a war over the control of the playground that was misfortunately situated between two architecturally identical buildings; our gang lived in one, the other gang in the other. The playground had swings and a slide, a merry-go-round and a sandbox, and was framed by bushes in which we liked to store stolen things and hide when hiding was required—the bushes were our *loga*, our base. The Playground War had a remarkable intensity, with many battles fought; there would be dozens of kids in each army, crowding the playground, using sticks as cudgels to their pain-inflicting maximum. I recalled for Alma raising high my grandfather's walking stick to crash it through a cardboard shield that another kid put up as his pitifully feeble protection. We lost the final battle and the rights to the playground when the enemy army received reinforcements from two eighth-graders on their way to school: they swung their book-heavy bags with murderous delight and mowed us mightily as we retreated in disarray.

So we had to relocate our *loga*—our flags, our armory, our pride—to the garden behind our building. The garden was rather large and belonged to the old people who lived in the house at the far end of it. The house was decrepit; the walls had large water stains, resembling old maps of imagined oceans; the shingles would simply and suddenly slide off the roof. Before the Playground War, we seldom ventured there, for we were wary of the old people, who would come out of the house and bark crazily: the old woman flung her arms around like a demented windmill; the old man waved his stick at us as if conducting a hallucinatory orchestra. They were clearly sick: both of them wore heavy vests and sweaters in the summer; their legs were swollen like tree stumps; the smell of rot and death wafted out of their windows when they, seldom, opened them. But the garden was a vast territory of potato and cabbage patches and little forests of pole beans and corn, where we could hide and replenish our supply of war sticks. In the fall there were pumpkins; in the spring there were the green bunny ears of young onions. In the winter, it all turned into a mud field, which would slow down any enemy suddenly charging at us; and if there was snow, we could build an unconquerable ice bunker. There was even an apple tree that we could use as an observation tower, on which we could hang our flag. It was hard to believe that we had not thought of the garden as the *loga* before.

So we invaded it and conquered it, ignoring, indeed taunting, the old couple whenever they tottered after us in ridiculously hopeless pursuit. At last they accepted the defeat; we threw a rock through their window, and there was nothing they could do. Pretty soon we were ripping out their cabbage heads and beating them to shreds with our sticks; we were killing lizards in our rock-throwing practice; we were immolating snails by pouring lighter fluid into their shells and igniting them. The garden was our liberated, sovereign territory now, our home turf.

"And how is this related to your American-commando phase?" Alma asked, somewhat brusquely.

"I'm getting to that," I said. "Be a patient young lady."

A few weeks later, a crew of men in blue overalls drove up in a big truck and started putting up a board fence around the garden. It didn't take them long to finish it, and we soon realized that we couldn't just walk in to get our sticks or collect sacrificial snails. When we eventually sneaked inside, we found out that the old people's house was roofless now; two sweaty men were tearing up the walls with sledgehammers; a bulldozer was lying in wait to turn it all into a nebulous pile. The following day, the workers completed the fencing off, and the garden was entirely out of bounds for us, the fence tall and surprisingly solid, devoid of cracks and holes. We could hear ditch-diggers and jackhammers and the din of demolition and construction, but we could not see what was happening inside. Suddenly we were banished from what had always been our rightful territory.

Finally, Vampir, being the youngest and the smallest of us, was hurled over the fence for a reconnaissance mission. We waited for his return at the steps of our building, passing around a cigarette, discussing, as we were wont to, masturbation and ways to die. He came back with a bleak report. The potato patch was gone, the apple tree was uprooted, the house was leveled, the bean poles and the corn were cut down; there was a huge hole in the ground, its edges marked by stakes connected with a rope on which yellow flags were hung. Djordje thought that was because they had mined it all. There was a brigade of heavy machinery scattered all around, Vampir went on. And near the gate, they were just about to complete a wooden barrack, with doors and windows, obviously their future headquarters. They had no intention of leaving, Vampir said. We were going to make them leave, Djordje insisted, and they were going to regret ever coming.

In a message posted all over our building, we indicated that the situation was very serious. We summoned all the veterans of previous wars, all the kids who had enjoyed the garden of freedom, for a war council where we were to decide what to do. The congregating place was a basement storage room belonging to the fifth-floor homosexual. We had broken the lock and established our temporary headquarters there, knowing that he would never come down. The storage room was full of suitcases, which were full of old magazines, which were full of pictures of sunny seaside resorts and people on the beaches. The suitcases were stacked haphazardly, so they formed a kind of shaky amphitheater that could host a lot of kids. But only seven showed up: Djordje, Vampir, Boris, Edo, Mahir, myself, and inexplicably, Marina.

"What happened to them?" Alma asked.

"When?"

"In the war."

"Which war?"

"The real war."

"Oh, I don't know. I have to think about it."

Djordje was presiding; he presented the situation in the starkest overtones. The garden had been overridden by strangers who seemed to be building something in its stead. We had been expelled so many times before that we no longer had anyplace to go. If we lost the garden, there would be nothing we could call ours. If we let them build whatever they were building, the loss would be irreparable and irreversible. We had to do something, now, we all agreed. War seemed inevitable, but there were only seven of us. I proposed that we issue a warning to the Workers—as our enemy was called from then on—to tell them they had encroached upon our lawful territory and so they must leave without delay. The proposal was submitted for a vote, and it passed; the only one against was Djordje. (I was particularly pleased that Marina raised her dainty hand: she had raven-black hair and even darker eyes.) I was given the task of composing the letter of warning. I put my advanced literacy to work and wrote a preternaturally verbose missive using phrases such as "righteous wrath," "blood-soaked liberty," and "the course of justice." I signed it "The Insurgents," the name inspired by the history of Yugoslavia, whose many nationalities traditionally died in various freedom-seeking insurgencies.

The Insurgents was a name I had thought up without discussion or approval. Djordje disliked it, as did Edo. But I had written it in blood-red ink, for dramatic effect, and it had taken a few ink-stained drafts to get it right, so rewriting would have taken a long time. Besides, the name Djordje proposed—The Motherfuckers—was too much, most of us thought, as was the way he formulated our anger in his draft: "If you don't leave, we'll fuck your mothers and sisters and children." Thus it stayed as I wrote it, with the understanding that we could and should crank it up in the follow-up. We hurled Vampir over the fence again, and he spat on the back of the ultimatum and stuck it to the barrack door.

"Now, I have to ask," Alma said. "What do you mean when you say you hurled him over the fence?"

I don't like when people interrupt me; I like to tell stories as I see fit. But Alma asked firmly and, perhaps as an unconscious forewarning, looked into the camera's viewfinder. It was important to me that she liked me, that she understood my experience.

"Well, two of us would make a square with our forearms, grabbing each other's wrists"—I showed her, grasping her thin, fragile wrists lightly—"and then Vampir would step on it and we would throw him up on the fence. He was so light-footed, so limber and dexterous, that he could stand on the fence for a moment before jumping down on the other side."

"Why did you call him Vampir?"

"He had no body. He was so weightless that he left no footprints in the snow."

"What happened to him?"

I paused before I responded, and when I told her he had been shot by a sniper, in 1992, in front of our building, her face showed no emotion. I wondered if the word "sniper" necessarily brought up in her mind the killing of her mother, or her brother, whichever it was, so I hurried to continue the story.

In any case, the Workers did not leave. The next warning was written by Djordje, who threatened them with harsh motherfucking, overlooking the fact that fucking was not the strongest weapon of prepubescent boys. He gave them a week to leave, and to show them how serious we were, Vampir was to throw a rock through a barrack window after delivering the threat. But he stood too close to the window and merely cracked it; for all we knew, the Workers could have concluded that a sparrow crashed into it, breaking its neck.

It was a tactical error to issue all the threats, for instead of taking them seriously the Workers poured concrete into the hole in the ground and built a foundation for what looked like a huge building. Moreover, while we waited for their response, school was out, and we consequently lost Boris, Edo, and Marina, who were shipped off for the summer to their respective grandparents. Come to think of it, I can't remember why I was not shipped off to my grandparents' that summer.

"Because your mother was going through a treatment for ovarian cancer," Alma said.

That was news to me. I shook my head in disbelief; she nodded, confirming.

"How the hell do you know that? I've never heard of my mother having ovarian cancer."

"She told me."

"She told you? My mother? She told you about her cancer? Why didn't she tell me?"

"She didn't want you to worry."

Honestly, I don't know whether I would have worried, being busy with the Garden War and all. But my mother's cancer explained a lot. For example, it explained why I had been enrolled in a summer course of English, despite my strenuous objections—they had wanted me out of the house, yet close to them; they did not want me to know but could not let me go too far, to my grandparents'. And now I knew why I could stay out and dedicate the late summer nights to our war efforts, and why they had bought me a lot of unsolicited toys, including the rifle I loved so much, an AK-47 replica I mistook for an American weapon. They wanted me distracted, and distracted I was. It was because of my mother's cancer that I became the American commando. Imagine that.

Anyway, I hated the English classes. We had to sit in a small, hot room, the sun beating into the green shades, whole inhalable galaxies of dust particles levitating around us. I preferred observing their rotation and random movement to listening to a visibly bored teacher, who perked up only when we sang songs in English. We idiotically repeated the words she fed us, following her lead as she belted them out; it appeared her secret passion was to be a famous singer. We sang "My Bonnie Lies over the Ocean," "When Johnny Comes Marching Home," "Amazing Grace," songs I could not even hum now without retching. Her favorite, however, was "Catch a Falling Star." She translated the lyrics for us, and whenever she sang it she would reach out to catch the imaginary falling star and put it in her pocket. It was pathetic; we elbowed one another and giggled.

You see, I had acquired a rifle I loved, I was learning a language only I could speak, I had parents who left me alone—for whatever reason—and what I needed was the right identity that would absorb it all. I discovered it in the movie in which a small unit of American commandos destroyed a mountain serving as a secret weapons factory for the evil Germans. The slow-motion images of the apocalyptic blast greatly impressed me: the mountain belching before its top vanished in a cataclysm, the curlicues of fire emerging from the black-cotton-candy smoke, and then the peace of absolute destruction afterward, the ashes of oblivion floating down, the silence. And there was a beautiful scene in which an American commando was tortured by the Germans, and instead of breaking down under the duress, instead of selling out his buddies, he sang "Clementine." The movie was called *The Mountain of Doom*, and having seen it twice in two days, I began crawling on the carpeted floor of my room imagining it as a mossy mountain slope; I hid under the bed as if under a truck; I assumed shooting positions behind the furniture in wait for a German who did not know that his death was around the corner. Hence it was an obvious and natural step to become a sniper watching from my window a Worker pushing a wheelbarrow. I imagined a bullet entering and exiting his head, followed by a spurt of brain offal. At some point, I spoke to myself in what I thought was the American language, a distorted combination of the sounds I had picked up watching movies and singing in class, pronounced according to the rule that my father had once established: Unlike British English, which you pronounce as though your mouth were scalded with hot tea, American English requires chewing imaginary gum. *Fow dou sotion gemble*, I would say under my breath, my gun pointed at a Worker hosing down his rubber boots. *Fecking plotion, camman. Yeah, sure.*

My conversion into an American commando coincided nicely with the escalation of the armed struggle against the Workers. They had not left, of course, for they were well into raising the building, what with the steel rods sprouting out of the concrete and the first-floor walls being put up. When Djordje said that now was the time to fuck some mothers, nobody objected, and therefore the war was commenced.

Djordje became the commander in chief, the leader, focused and ruthless. Vampir was the Special Force, a spook who performed clandestine operations: he talked little, wore darker clothes than the rest of us, and acquired a penchant for sneaking up from behind. Mahir was the infantry, bravely obeying orders, ever reliable in combat. And I was the American commando, on a special mission to help the cause of freedom in the Garden War, well equipped with a real rifle, speaking fluently the chewing-gum American, even if I had to translate it constantly for my comrades.

The first engagement of the Garden War took place on a June evening. While most of the Workers had gone home, a few stayed behind to drink beer on the steps of the barrack with the Security Guard. They did not know that war was descending upon them; they were innocent of the enemy rattling their weapons within a stone's throw. In preparation for our first assault, we had dug a tunnel under the fence, then covered the exit hole with a plank and debris. The objective was to burn down one of the wooden sheds where the Workers kept their tools and rubber boots and overalls. That evening, we crawled inside through the tunnel, our pockets full of little lighter fluid containers, our bookless school bags full of old newspapers and rags. I had my rifle strapped to my back, so I got stuck under the fence, but the others managed to pull me out. While the Security Guard was getting wasted with his comrades, we ripped the tips of the plastic lighter-fluid containers with our teeth, then soaked the bunched-up newspapers and rags piled against the back of the shed farthest from the barrack. As we lit the pile, the Workers laughed in dear oblivion. Then we raced toward the tunnel and crawled out. Even if my heart was performing a drum solo, I had the presence of mind to have my gun in my hand. According to the plan, we scattered and went to our respective homes. By the time I was up at my window, one corner of the shed was wildly aflame and the Security Guard and his buddies were stupidly sprinkling the fire with their beer, until the least drunk one among them stretched a hose from the spigot and put the flames out.

I always enjoyed destruction; there was always something breathtaking in effecting obliteration. I had been prone to laying waste: I had liked to take a hammer to a toy car or to drop marbles from my balcony and see them explode on the pavement. I had torn pages, one by one, out of a book I disliked, until there was nothing but the meaningless cover. After all, I had even enjoyed wiping the chalkboard clean. But I had never been remotely as elated as when I watched that shed burning, when I witnessed the idiotic helplessness of the Security Guard spraying the inferno with his beer. And we knew that it was but a rehearsal for taking down the skyscraper, once they completed it—in the blaze of the shed fire I could see the Building of Doom collapsing unto itself.

It didn't matter that the shed was an actual outhouse. We watched the Workers retching and pinching their noses as they kicked the torched walls in, exposing an impressive mountain of shit. For a while afterward, the Workers, their bowels irritated with whatever bile they were served out of a large vat at lunchtime, scurried over to squat behind a stack of steel beams, clutching their communal roll of toilet paper. We had plenty to feel victorious about: A shithouse was a legitimate target, impeding the logistics of the building construction, not to mention that we had gotten behind the line of an enemy who didn't even know what had hit them. When we reconvened a couple of days later, I said: *Fatch ah salling frow, sure yeah, fut ow gnore tocket,* which I helpfully translated as: "The next thing, my friends, is the barrack."

We needed a lot of lighter fluid for the barrack. Collecting the little containers—the torpedo-shaped, finger-sized things—would have taken forever and would have cost too much. We had been stealing a lot of money from our parents' wallets to finance the Garden War, and the guy at the newspaper stand had already asked Mahir whether his dad was running his car on lighter fluid. Djordje assessed that a few cans of gasoline or some other flammable liquid would suffice. We broke into more storage rooms looking for something combustible that someone may have unwisely put away with some old pillows and rugs. We found no fuel, but there were a lot of coats, picture frames, defunct vacuum cleaners, old records and books, disintegrating furniture— the detritus of paltry existence. I could not imagine that anyone would have ever noticed or cared if it were to burn down.

And as I was saying that, I noticed Alma scanning my office: the plastic cups blooming with blunt pencils; a malachite ashtray; a cameraless lens; a bowl full of international change, collected on my writerly peregrinations; unframed pictures pinned to the corkboard above my desk, fading and curling upon themselves.

"You know, when I went back to Sarajevo for the first time after the war," she said, "I had to clean out my parents' apartment so I could sell it. So I made three piles of stuff: one to throw away, one to give away, and one to take with me to New York. The New York one fit into a suitcase. When I got back home, I put the suitcase in a storage room and haven't opened it since."

But see, for us, the war was elating, the freedom inherent in erasure, the absolute righteousness of our cause—we loved it all. Everything looked more beautiful from the top of the Mountain of Doom. And the life of stealth and deception, the feeling that we always knew far more than the people around us. Now we were courteous to our neighbors, deferential to the elderly; I did my English homework regularly, volunteered to sing in class. I knew that the pretending, the sacrifice, would help me perform my duty; the lies were an essential part of our mission. I found pride and beauty in self-denial, and finally understood what my parents meant when they said, "Sometimes you have to do things you hate doing." Even if they meant it in relation to being forced to have haircuts or to wash the car with my dad.

And after our good-boy performances we would get together in the basement and plot the Great Attack. Djordje thought that we ought to keep pressure on the Workers, never let them rest, while we were preparing for Doomsday. So as our parents imagined that we were playing marbles or watching a Disney movie at Kino Arena, we were wrapping sand and crushed glass into newspaper sheets that we would wet before the action. We called that weapon the Grenade; it was my invention, the idea being that the wet paper would break upon impact, and the sand mixed with glass would stick to the skin, and when the Worker tried to wipe it he would cut himself or scrape his skin off. And if we got him in the eyes, he could lose his eyes.

We threw Grenades and rocks at the Workers; we scattered nails at the truck entrance; we stuck matches into the barrack locks; we lit up lighter-fluid containers and cast them randomly across the fence. And as the building progressed, we refined our tactics. We learned that to attack the Workers was not prudent: there were too many of them, their movement was unpredictable, they far outnumbered us, and by now they worked high up inside the building. Therefore, the Security Guard became our main target. When others worked, he lingered around the barrack, opening and closing the gate for the trucks—he was often within a Grenade throw. He had a globular wart on his left cheek, which stuck out even if he was unshaven; there were dandruff droppings on his sloped shoulders. He wore a dun uniform, and a cap with a required red star that would have given him soldierly authority if it hadn't been so filthy—we had seen him wiping the sweat on his neck with it. In the evenings, he was alone, unless he had talked some Workers into staying and drinking with him, but even then, they would go home sooner or later. He didn't seem to have a home; we watched him wandering around the construction site languidly; I would have him pinpointed with my rifle as he sat at the barrack steps staring into some invisible distance—with a real weapon, one easy shot would have sufficed. Sometimes he would pull out a kitchen rag and unwrap it and take a piece of bread and some meat out of it; he munched detachedly, without appetite, as though the purpose of chewing was to make his jaw less lonely. God knows what he was thinking about; most likely it was nothing. We often caught him unawares and pelted him with rocks and Grenades, but had few direct hits.

For the longest time, he could not figure out who or what was after him; people like that take their own suffering to be a condition of their existence. Once he innocently bought a naked-lady magazine from Djordje, who went to the gate and called him over; we were supposed to attack him at that moment, but decided instead that his money would be more useful to us. He did not recognize that he was at war: we enjoyed watching his confusion, his vague, passive awareness that he was surrounded by the usual malice; we reveled in the fact that he didn't know who we were, *what* we were.

But as stupid as he was, the Guard eventually caught on. In fact, he nearly captured Vampir, who was writing messages featuring fucking, mothers, sisters, and children on the barrack. He sneaked up on him from behind, and started punching him, but Vampir managed to wriggle out of his hands and take off over the fence in a blink. We orchestrated a revenge attack immediately thereafter. We pelted the Guard with paper bags full of pebbles—Cluster Bombs—

and had a few handsome direct hits. He cursed at us with venom and hatred, and after that, it was clear the war was to be fought until one side suffered a consummate defeat.

And around that time we suddenly recognized we had long abandoned the hope of regaining the garden. We would not have been more satisfied if somehow, miraculously, the sovereignty of the garden was restored. Indeed, we would have lost our purpose. All we ever thought or talked about was how we could hurt the Workers as personified by the Security Guard; that was what the goal of the war had become, and we could imagine nothing before, after, or beyond it. It was like being in love, except we wanted to kill him. Beside the obliteration of the skyscraper, our dominant fantasy became torching the barrack while the Security Guard was in it.

For that, we needed fuel. One day, we lucked out: a picture frame shop by the train station burned down. We saw the smoke rising, we heard the howling of the sirens. Ever interested in ruination, we rushed over and watched the firemen douse the shop through the shattered front windows, while the owners, a husband and wife, wept and embraced, trying not to look at it. We went back to the smoldering shop the following day, walked over the warm ashes, here and there mushed up into cinereous mud, and inhaled the smell of charred wood and scorched mortar. We sifted through the rubble of the owners' lives: a woman's shoe with its heel completely melted; half a chair, leaning on the absent leg; frame corners still on the wall, still symmetrical. In the back of the shop was an unburnt corner: a stained blue overcoat still hanging; a framed picture of a wedded couple, facing the ceiling; and right by the back door, three beautiful cans of paint thinner. *Sengson clotion wicklup*, I said. We got what we needed.

Let me confess: I was perfectly aware that there was something inappropriate in my telling this story to Alina with so much pleasure. She must have found the boys entirely and typically aggressive, violent, and silly; she could have been hurt by the ease of their blood thirst. She was certainly not someone who could see the beauty in war, but she expressed no dismay—in fact, she showed no emotion at all. Occasionally, she looked into the little screen and adjusted the camera because I had wriggled over to the edge of the frame. And I am submitting that I was—how shall I put it—perversely amplifying certain details so as to elicit some reaction from her, to see her feel. But she was as stoic as her digital video camera.

"Do you want to take a break?" she said. "You've been talking for an hour."

"No, not at all," I said. "I like talking. I can talk forever."

One evening, we sneaked the cans through the tunnel, the mud from the day's rain soiling, possibly clogging up, my rifle. We scurried over to the hidden space between the barrack and the fence. We planned to soak with paint thinner the walls of the barrack in which the Guard was sleeping, make an inflammable puddle before the front door, so as to cut off his escape route, and then set it all ablaze. It should have been an easy mission; it should have lasted only a couple of minutes, but numbed by adrenaline, dazed by the danger, we did not think clearly—nobody had matches. Mahir was sent to fetch some while we waited in our hiding space, our courage draining by the moment.

Within a few minutes, Djordje became antsy and decided to go look for Mahir. I knew then that he would not come back, but I said nothing. Vampir and I slouched in silence, waiting for the time to pass so we could propose retreat. But then we heard the barrack floor creaking; the Guard stepped out, and stretched his arms toward the setting sun, roaring with a yawn. In an instant, he was going to turn around and see us and the cans. Before I could even think of making a move, Vampir darted past him toward the tunnel, and the Guard turned around to face me, as I stood paralyzed with the muddy rifle in my hands. What are you doing here? he asked me. *Geffle creel debbing,* I said. *Vau shetter bei doff. Camman.*

It is hard to explain why I was speaking the chewing-gum American to him. Perhaps because I thought, in panic, that if I still pretended to be an American I might convince him that I was a foreigner, that I was there by mistake and therefore innocent, and he would let me go. Or because I was, in fact, an American commando at that moment, thinking—if that is the word—that if I stayed inside my identity he would not be able to reach across the reality gap and punch me in the face, as he did, several times in a row. I put up my rifle against his fist, but he went around it, as I yelped: *Fetch a kalling star and pet it de packet, maike it for it meny dey.* And I kept repeating it, until it turned back into a song, as the Guard was raining blows on my head.

But the singing-under-torture did not help me at all in that moment. I fell to the ground and the Guard now tried to kick me in the head, while I tried to protect it with my arms. I have no doubt he would have killed me if he hadn't been distracted by a beer bottle flying at him. As he looked up, another one smashed into his forehead and exploded, and a shower of blood poured over me and the Guard fell down on his knees. I thought we had finally killed him. I was overcome with the joy of salvation and survival.

"Your parents did not tell me any of this," Alma said. I wished she had stopped looking at the little screen.

"They did not know," I said. "Nobody knew. We were a cabal, as they say, loyal only to each other. I've never told this to anybody."

"I see," she said. She didn't seem to have entirely suspended her disbelief.

So I escaped; Vampir saved me. The Guard was not, in fact, killed. While we ran home, he went inside the barrack and found a rag to press against the wound. Some minutes later, from my window, I watched him stagger through the gate, stand in front of it, look up (I ducked), and then heard him howl with pain and fury such as I had never heard before and never would hear again. He was not producing any words; he was inarticulate with rage and helplessness, bellowing like a wounded beast. I was thoroughly terrified, for I knew he would have without any doubt killed me if he could have laid his hands on me at that moment.

It was then, Alma, that the world became a dangerous place for me. Perhaps that is why my parents remember that period fondly—I spent a lot of time with them, seeking, unbeknownst to them, their protection. At the end of that summer, we went to the seaside for vacation and I obeyed the infamous whistle. When school started, for months I was afraid to leave our home alone, and they had to walk me to school and back. I returned to their fold; I returned home after the war.

And while Alma was glancing at the camera, I realized that pretty soon, my mother and my father would die and that, even though it had been long since they had protected me from anything, I would be left alone and exposed to the world, devoid of home and love, left alone to confront all the people full of pain and anger. I thought of the day way back in grammar school when I had gone to wet the chalkboard sponge, and in the empty hallway there stood my parents, looking for a teacher's room. Usually, only one of them would come for a conference with a teacher, but this time, they were together; I seem to remember them holding hands. They looked big in comparison with all the little lockers, the children's shoes lined up; they grinned when they saw me, proud of me clutching a sponge, performing duties. I felt that the three of us were together; we were inside, and everyone else—the kids in the classrooms, the teachers—was outside. They kissed me; I went back to my classroom; they went to wait for the teacher.

"And that's it," I told Alma. "That's the end of the story. Now we can take a break."

"That's great. I could probably use that," she said, not sounding convinced. "But could you speak a little more in your chewing-gum American? Can you still do it? I'd like to have you speak American and Bosnian in the film. Could you do that for me?"

"Sure," I said. *"Floxon thay formtion. Camman, dey flai prectacion. Gnow aut sol, lone. Yeah, sure."*

The Noble Truths of Suffering

The uniformed *jaran* did not acknowledge that I spoke in Bosnian to him. Silently, he checked my invitation, then compared the picture in my American passport with my mopey local face, and it appeared to have matched reasonably well. His head resembled an armchair- -the deep-set forehead, the handlebar-like ears, the jutted jaw-seat—and I could not stop staring at it. He handed me back my passport with the invitation tucked inside and said, with his furniture-head accent: "Good evening to you."

The American ambassador's house was a huge ugly new thing, famously built high up in the hills by a Bosnian tycoon before he abruptly decided he needed even more space and, without spending a day in it, rented it to His American Excellency. There was still some work to be done—the narrow concrete path zigzagged meaninglessly through a veritable mud field; the bottom left corner of the frontage was unpainted, so it looked like a recently scarred-over wound. Farther up the hill, one could see a yellow lace threading the fringes of the woods, marking a wilderness thick with mines.

Inside, however, all was asparkle. The walls were dazzling white, the stairs squeaked with untroddenness; on the first landing was a stand with a large bronze eagle, its wings frozen mid-flap over a hapless, writhing snake. At the top of the stairs, in a spiffy suit, if a size too big, stood Jonah, the cultural attaché, whom I had once misaddressed as Johnny and kept misaddressing since, pretending it was a joke. "Johnny-boy," I said, "how goes it?" He shook my hand wholeheartedly, claiming he was extremely happy to see me. And maybe he was, who am I to say.

I snatched a glass of beer and a flute of champagne from a tray-carrying mope whose Bosnianness was unquestionably signified by a crest of hair looming over his forehead. "*Šta ima?*" I said. "*Evo,*" he said. "*Radim.*" I downed the beer and washed it down with champagne before I entered the already crowded mingle room. I tracked down another tray-holder, who despite a mustached leathery face looked vaguely familiar, like someone who may have bullied me in high school. "*Šta ima?*" I asked. "*Evo,*" he said. "*Ništa.*"

Ambidextrously armed with more beer and champagne, I assumed a corner position from which I could, cougarlike, monitor the gathering. I spotted the minister of culture, resembling a bald, mangy panda, despite the fact that all the fingers on both of his hands were individually bandaged—he held his champagne flute between his palms like a votive candle. There were various Bosnian TV personalities, sporting their Italian spectacles and the telegenic abundance of unnecessary frowns and smirks. The writers were recognizable by the incoherence bubbling up on their stained-tie surfaces. A throng of Armani-clad businessmen swarmed around the pretty, young interpreters, while the large head of a famous retired basketball player hovered over them like a full moon. I spotted the ambassador—stout, prim, Republican, with a small, puckered-asshole mouth—talking to someone who must have been Macalister. The possible Macalister was in a purple velvet jacket over a Hawaiian shirt; his denim pants were worn out and bulging at the knees, as though he spent his days kneeling; he wore open-toe Birkenstocks with white socks; everything on him looked hand-me-down. He was in his fifties but had a head of Bakelite-black hair, so unyielding it seemed it had been mounted on his head decades before and had not changed its form since. Without expressing any identifiable emotion, he was listening to the ambassador, who was rocking back on his heels, pursing his lips, slowly passing out a thought. Macalister was drinking water; his glass slanted slightly in his hand so the water edge repeatedly touched the brim only to retreat, in the exact rhythm of the ambassador's rocking. I was already tipsy enough to be able to accost Macalister as soon as the ambassador left him alone. I finished my beer and champagne and was considering pursuit of a tray for the purpose of refueling, when the ambassador bellowed: "May I have your attention, please!" and the din quieted down, and the tray mopes stopped moving, and the crowd around the ambassador and Macalister spread away a bit.

"It is my great pleasure and privilege," the ambassador vociferated, rocking in a very slow rhythm, "to welcome Dick Macalister, our great writer and—based on the little time I have spent talking to him—an even greater guy."

We all applauded obediently. Macalister was looking down at his empty glass. He moved it from hand to hand, then slipped it into his pocket.

Some weeks before, I had received an invitation from the United States ambassador to Bosnia and Herzegovina, His Excellency Eliot Auslander, to join him in honoring Richard Macalister, a Pulitzer Prize winner and acclaimed author. The invitation was sent to my Sarajevo address, only a week or so after I had arrived. I could not figure out how the embassy knew I was there, though I had a few elaborately paranoid ideas. It troubled me greatly that I was located as soon as I landed, for I came to Sarajevo for shelter. My plan was to stay at our family apartment for a few months and forget about a large number of things (my divorce, my breakdown, the War on Terror, everything) that had tormented me in Chicago. My parents were already in Sarajevo for their annual spring stay, and my sister was to join us upon her return from New Zealand; hence the escape to Sarajevo was beginning to feel like a depleted déjà vu of our previous life. We were exactly where we had been before the war, but everything was fantastically different—we were different; the neighbors were fewer and different; the hallway smell was different; and from our window we could see a ruin that used to be a kindergarten and now nobody cared to raze.

I wasn't going to go to the reception; I had had enough of America and Americans to last me for another lousy lifetime. But my parents were very proud that the American ambassador was willing to welcome me at his residence. The invitation—the elaborate coat of arms, the elegant cursive, the volutes and whorls of His Excellency's signature—

recalled for them the golden years of my father's diplomatic service and officially elevated me into the realm of respectable adults. Father offered to let me wear his suit to the reception; he claimed it still looked good, despite its being twenty or so years old and sporting a triangular iron burn on its lapel.

I kept resisting their implorations until I went to an Internet café to read up on Richard Macalister. I had heard of him, of course, but had never read any of his books, as I seldom read contemporary American fiction. With an emaciated teenager to my left liquidating scores of disposable video-game civilians and a cologne-reeking gentleman to my right listlessly browsing bestiality sites, I surfed through the life and work of Dick Macalister. To cut a long story short, he was born, he lived, he wrote books, he inflicted suffering and occasionally suffered himself. In *Fall*, his most recent memoir—"a heartbreaking, clenched-jaw confession"--he owned up to his wife-abusing, extended drinking binges, and spectacular breakdowns. In the novel *Depth Sickness*, a loan shark shot off his foot on a hunting trip, then redeemed in recollection his vacuous, vile life while waiting for help or death, both of which arrived at approximately the same time. "Macalister seems to have never heard of the dissociation of sensibilities," *The New York Times* eulogized, "for his book is a host to a whole slew of them." I skimmed the reviews of the short story collections (one of them was called *Suchness*) and spent time reading about *Nothing We Say*, "Macalister's masterpiece," the winner of a Pulitzer Prize for Fiction. The novel was about "a

Vietnam vet who does everything to get out of war, but cannot get war out of himself." Everybody was crazy about it. "It is hard not to be humbled by the honest brutality of Macalister's tortured heroes," one reviewer wrote. "These men speak little not because they have nothing to say but because the last remnants of decency in their dying hearts compel them to protect others from what they could say." It all sounded pretty good to me, but nothing to write home about. I found a Macalister fan site, where there was a selection of passages from his works accompanied by pages upon pages of trivial exegesis. Some of the quotations were rather nice, and I wrote them down:

Before Nam, Cupper was burdened with the pointless enthusiasm of youth.

The best remedy for the stormy sky is a curtain, he said.

On the other side of the vast, milky windowpane there sauntered a crew of basketball players, their shadows like a caravan passing along the horizon.

Cupper had originally set out to save the world, but now he knew it was not worth it.

One of these days the thick chitin of the world will break open, and shit and sorrow will pour out and drown us all. Nothing we say can stop that.

I liked that one. *The thick chitin of the world,* that was pretty good.

We all eagerly drank to Macalister's health and success, whereupon he was beset by a swarm of the quickest suck-ups. I stepped out to the balcony, where all the smokers were forced to congregate. I pretended I was looking for someone, stretching my neck, squinting, but whoever I was looking for did not seem to be there. Down in the valley were dotted-light streets and illuminated, rocketlike minarets; at the far fringe of the night, toward Mojmilo hill, the pitch at the Željo soccer stadium was heartbreakingly green. Nothing was moving down below, as though the city were sunk at the bottom of a sea.

When I went back in, Macalister was talking to a woman with long auburn hair, her fingers lasciviously curved around a champagne flute. The woman was Bosnian, identifiable by her meaty carmine lips and a cluster of darkened-silver necklaces and a ruby pendant struggling to sink into her bosom, and the way she touched his forearm when she spoke to him; for all I knew, I could have had a hopeless crush on her in high school. She somehow managed to smile and laugh at the same time, her brilliant teeth an annotation to her laughter, her hair merrily flitting around. Macalister was burning to fuck her—I could tell from the way he leaned into her, his snout nearly touching her hair, sniffing her. It was jealousy, to be perfectly honest, that made me overcome my stage fright the moment the laughing woman was distracted by an embassy flunky. As she turned away from Macalister, I barged right in and wedged myself between the two of them.

"So what brings you to Sarajevo?" I asked. He was shorter than I; I could smell his hairiness, a furry, feral smell. His water glass was in his hand again, still empty.

"I go places," he said, "because there are places to go."

He had the sharp-edged nose of an ascetic. Every now and then the muscles at the root of his jaw tightened. He kept glancing at the woman behind me, who was laughing yet again.

"I'm on a State Department tour," he added, thereby ruining the purity of his witticism. "And on assignment for a magazine."

"So how do you like Sarajevo?"

"Haven't seen much of it yet, but it reminds me of Beirut."

But what about the Gazi Husrevbegova fountain, whose water tastes like no other in the world? What about all the minarets lighting up simultaneously at sunset on a Ramadan day? And the snow falling slowly, each flake coming down patiently, separately, as if abseiling down an obscure silky thread? What about the morning clatter of wooden shutters in Baščaršija, when all the old stores are opening at the same time and the streets smell of thick-foamed coffee? The chitin of the world is still hardening here, buddy.

I get emotional when inebriated. I said none of the above, however. Instead, I said:

"I've never been in Beirut."

Macalister glanced at the woman behind my back, flashing a helpless smile. The woman laughed liltingly, the glasses chinked; as always, the good life was elsewhere.

"I could show you some things in Sarajevo, things no tourist could see."

"Sure," Macalister said without conviction. I introduced

myself and proceeded to deliver the usual, well-rehearsed story of displacement and writing in English, nudging him toward declaring whether he had read me or not. He nodded and smiled. He was not as committed to our conversation as I was.

"You may have read my story 'Love and Obstacles,'" I said. "It was in *The New Yorker* not so long ago."

"Oh yeah, 'Love and Obstacles.' Great story," he said. "Will you excuse me?"

And so he left me for the red-haired woman. I guzzled the champagne and the beer, then grabbed the only glass left on a fleeting tray—it was watered-down whiskey, but it would do. The woman's hair was dyed anyway.

I kept relieving the tray-carriers of their loads. I talked to the basketball player, looking up at him until my neck hurt, inquiring unremittingly about the shot he had missed a couple of decades earlier, the shot that deprived his team of the national title and, I believed, commenced the general decline of Sarajevo. I cornered the minister of culture in order to find out what had happened to his fingers—his wife's dress had caught fire in the kitchen and he had had to strip it off her. I giggled. She had ended up with second-degree burns, he said. At some point, I tracked down my friend Johnny to impart to him that you can't work for the U.S. government unless you are a certified asshole, to which he grinned and said, "I could get you a job tomorrow," which I thought was not unfunny. Before I exited, I bade good-bye to Eliot Auslander by slapping him on the back and startling him, and then turned that fucking eagle to face the wall, the unfortunate consequence of which was that the snake was now hopelessly cornered. Best of luck, little reptile.

The air outside was adrizzle. The ambassador's house was way the fuck up the hill, and you had to go downhill to get anywhere. The flunkies were summoning cabs, but I wanted to air my head out, so downhill I went. The street was narrow, with no sidewalks, the upper floors of ancient houses leaning over the pavement. Across the valley, there was the caliginous Trebević; through a street-level window I saw a whole family sitting on a sofa, watching the weather forecast on TV—the sun stuck, like a coin, into a cloud floating over the map of Bosnia. I passed a peaceful police station and a freshly dead pigeon; a torn, faded poster on a condemned house announced a new CD by a bulbous half-naked singer, who, rumor had it, was fucking both the prime minister and the deputy prime minister. A tattered cat that looked like a leprechaun dog crossed my path. I turned the corner and saw, far ahead, Macalister and the redhead strolling toward the vanishing point, her hair brushing her shoulders as she turned to him to listen, his hand occasionally touching the small of her back to guide her around potholes and puddles.

I was giddy, scurrying up, thinking of funny things to say, my mind never quite reaching over to the other, funny side. I was giddy and drunk, slipping on the wet pavement and in need of company, and I trotted downhill after them, slipping, yet lucidly avoiding the holes and litter and a garbage container in which garbage quietly smoldered. Once I caught up with them, I just assumed their pace and walked along as straight as I could, saying nothing, which was somehow supposed to be funny too. Macalister uttered an unenthusiastic "Hey, you're okay?" and the woman said, *"Dobro veče,"* with a hesitation in her voice that suggested that I was interrupting something delectable and delicate. I just kept walking, skidding and stumbling, but in control, I was in control, I was. I did not know where we were, but they seemed to be headed somewhere.

"Anyway," Macalister said. "There is blowing of the air, but there is no wind that does the blowing."

"What wind?" I said. "There's no wind."

"There is a path to walk on, there is walking being done, but there is no walker."

"That is very beautiful," the woman said, smiling. She exuded a nebula of mirth. All of her consonants were as soft as the underside of a kitten's paw.

"There are deeds being done, but there is no doer," Macalister went on.

"What the hell are you talking about?" I asked. The toes of his white socks were caked with filth now.

"Malo je on puk'o," I suggested to the woman.

"Nije, baš lijepo zbori," she said. "It is poetry."

"It's from a Buddhist text," he said.

"It is beautiful," the woman said.

"There is drizzle and there is shit to be rained on, but there is no sky," I pronounced.

"That could work too," Macalister said.

The drizzle made the city look begrimed. A couple of glistening umbrellas cascaded downhill toward the scarce traffic flow of Titova Street. At the low end of Dalmatinska, you would take a right, then walk straight for about ten minutes, past Veliki Park and the Alipašina mosque, past the fenced-off vacant lot where the old hospital used to be, and then you reached Marin Dvor, and across the street from the ruin that used to be the tobacco factory used to be the building where I was born.

"You're okay, Macalister," I said. "You're a good guy. You're not an asshole."

"Why, thank you," Macalister said. "I'm glad I've been vetted."

We reached the bottom of Dalmatinska and stopped there. Had I not been there, Macalister would have suggested to the woman that they spend more time together, perhaps in his hotel room, perhaps attached at the groin. But I was there and I wasn't leaving, and there was an awkward silence as they waited for me to at least step away so they could exchange poignant parting words. I snapped the silence and suggested that we all go out for a drink. Macalister looked straight into her eyes and said, "Yeah, let's go out for a drink," his gaze doubtless conveying that they could ditch me quickly and continue their discussion of Buddhism and groin attachment. But the woman said no, she had to go home, she was really tired, she had to go to work early, she'd love to but she was tired, no, sorry. She shook my hand limply and gave Macalister a hug, in the course of which she pressed her sizable chest against his. I did not even know her name. She went toward Marin Dvor.

"What's her name?" I asked.

Macalister watched her wistfully as she ran to catch an approaching streetcar.

"Azra," he said.

"Let's have a drink," I said. "You've got nothing else to do anyway, now that Azra's gone."

Honestly, I would have punched me in the face, or at least hurled some hurtful insults my way, but not only did Macalister not do it, he did not express any hostility whatsoever and agreed to come along for a drink. It must have been his Buddhist thing or something.

We went toward Baščaršija—I pointed out to him the Eternal Fire, which was supposed to be burning for the antifascist liberators of Sarajevo, but happened to be out at the moment; then, farther down Ferhadija, we stopped at the site of the 1992 bread-line massacre, where there was a heap of wilted flowers; then passed Writers' Park, where busts of important Bosnian authors were hidden behind stalls offering pirate DVDs. We passed the cathedral, then Egipat, which made the best ice cream in the world, then the Gazi Husrevbegova mosque and the fountain. I told him about the song that asserted that once you drank Baščaršija water you would never forget Sarajevo. We drank the water; he lapped it out of the palm of his small hand, the water splattering his white socks.

"I love your white socks, Macalister," I said. "When you

take them off, don't throw them away. Give them to me. I'll keep them as a relic, smell them for good luck whenever I write."

"I never take them off," he said. "That's my only pair."

For a moment, I considered the possibility that he was serious, for his delivery was deadpan, no crack signals in the air. It seemed he was looking out at me and the city from an interior space no other human had access to. I did not know exactly where we were going, but he did not complain or ask questions, as though it didn't matter, because he would always be safe inside himself. I confess: I wanted him be in awe of Sarajevo, of me, of what we meant in the world; I wanted to break through to him, through his chitin.

But I was hungry and needed a drink or two, so instead of wandering all night, we ended up in a smoky basement restaurant whose owner, Faruk, was a war hero—there was a shoulder missile-launcher hanging high up on the brick wall, and pictures of uniformed men below it. I knew Faruk pretty well, for he had dated my sister many years before. He greeted us, spread apart the rope curtain leading into the dining room and took us to our table, next to a glass case with a shiny black gun and a holster.

"*Ko ti je to?*" Faruk asked as we sat down.

"*Pisac. Amerikanac. Dobio Pulitzera,*" I said.

"*Pulitzer je dosta jak,*" Faruk said, and offered his hand to Macalister: "Congratulations."

Macalister thanked him, but when Faruk walked away, he noted the preponderance of weapons.

"Weapons schmeapons," I said. "The war is over. Don't worry about it."

A waiter, who looked like a twin brother of one of the tray mopes, came by, and I ordered a trainload of food—all varieties of overcooked meat and fried dough—and a bottle of wine, without asking Macalister what he would like. He was vegetarian and didn't drink, he said impassively, merely stating a fact.

"So you're a Buddhist or something?" I said. "You don't step on ants and roaches, you don't swallow midges and such?"

He smiled. I had known Macalister for only a few hours, but I already knew he did not get angry. How can you write a book—how can you write a single goddamn sentence—without getting angry? I wondered. How do you even wake up in the morning without getting angry? I get angry in my dreams, wake up furious. He merely shrugged at my questions. I drank more wine and then some more, and whatever coherence I may have regained on our walk was quickly gone. I showered him with questions: Did he serve in Vietnam? How much of his work was autobiographical? Was Cupper his alter ego? Was it over there that he had become a Buddhist? What was getting the Pulitzer like? Did he ever have a feeling that this was all shit—this: America, humankind, writing, everything? And what did he think of Sarajevo? Did he like it? Could he see how beautiful it had been before it became this cesspool of insignificant, drizzly suffering?

Macalister talked to me, angerlessly. Occasionally I had a hard time following him, not least because Faruk sent over another bottle, allegedly his best wine, and I kept swilling it. Macalister had been in Vietnam, he had experienced nothing ennobling there. He was not Buddhist, he was "Buddhistish." And the Pulitzer made him vainglorious—"vainglorious" was the word he used—and now he was ashamed of it all a bit; any serious writer ought to be humiliated and humbled by fame. When he was young, like me, he said, he used to think that all the great writers knew something he didn't. He thought that if he read their books they would teach him something, make him better; he thought he would acquire what they had: the wisdom, the truth, the wholeness, the real shit. He was burning to write, he wanted to break through to that fancy knowledge, he was hungry for it. But now he knew that that hunger was vainglorious; now he knew that writers knew nothing, really; most of them were just faking it. He knew nothing. There was nothing to know, nothing on the other side. There was no walker, no path, just walking. This was it, whoever you were, wherever you were, whatever it was, and you had to make peace with that fact.

"This?" I asked. "What is 'this'?"

"This. Everything."

"Fuck me."

He talked more and more as I was sinking into oblivion, slurring the few words of concession and agreement and fascination I could utter. I would not remember most of the things he talked about, but as drunk as I was, it was clear to me that his sudden, sincere verbosity was due to his sense that our encounter—our writerly one-night stand—was a fleeting one. He even helped me totter up the stairs as we were leaving the restaurant, and flagged a cab for me. But I would not get into it, no sir, before he believed me that I would read all of his books, all of them, all that he had written, hack magazine jobs, blurbs, everything, and when he finally believed, I wanted him to swear that he would come over to my place, have lunch at my home with me and my parents, because he was family now, one of us, he was an honorary Sarajevan, and I made him write down our phone number and promise that he would call, tomorrow, first thing in the morning. I would have made him promise some other things, but the street cleaners were approaching with their blasting hoses and the cabdriver honked impatiently and I had to go, and off I went, drunk and high on bonding with one of the greatest writers of our embarrassing shit-ass time. By the time I arrived home, I didn't think I would ever see him again.

But he called, ladies and gentlemen of prestigious literary prize committees; to his eternal credit he kept his promise and called the very next morning, as I was staring at the ceiling, my eyeballs bobbling on a hangover scum pond. It was not even ten o'clock, for Buddha's sake, yet Mother walked into my room, bent over the floor mattress to enter my painful field of vision and give me the handset without a word. When he said, "It's Dick," I frankly did not know what he was talking about. "Dick Macalister," he said; it took me a moment to remember who he was. Furthermore, it felt as though I had returned to America and the whole Sarajevo escape was but a limp dream, and in short, I was afraid.

"So at what time should I come over?" he asked.

"Come over where?"

"Come over for lunch."

Let me skip all the uhms and ahms and all the words I fumbled as I struggled to reassemble my thinking apparatus, until I finally and arbitrarily selected the three-o'clock hour as our lunchtime. There was no negotiation. Richard Macalister was coming to eat my mother's food; he offered no explanation or reason; he did not sound excessively warm or excited. I did not think that anything that had happened the night before could lead to any friendship, substantial or otherwise—the most I could ever hope for was a future tepid blurb from him. I had no idea what it was that he might want from us. But I spelled out our address for him so he could give it to a cabbie, warned him against paying more than ten convertible marks, and told him that the building was right behind the kindergarten ruin. I hung up the phone; Dick Macalister was coming.

In my pajamas I stood exposed to the glare of my parents' morning judgment (they did not like it when I drank) and, with the aid of a handful of aspirin, informed them that Richard Macalister, an august American author, a winner of a Pulitzer Prize, an abstemious vegetarian, and a serious candidate for a full-time Buddhist, was coming over for lunch at three o'clock. After a moment of silent discombobulation, my mother reminded me that our regular lunchtime was one-thirty. But when I shrugged to indicate helplessness, she sighed and went on to inspect the supplies in the fridge and the freezer chest. Presently she started issuing deployment orders: my father was to go to the produce market with a list, right now; I was to brush my teeth and, before any coffee or breakfast, hurry to the supermarket to buy bread, kefir, or whatever it was that vegetarians drank, and also vacuum cleaner bags; she was going to start preparing pie dough. By the time she was clearing the table where she would spread the dough and thin it out with a rolling pin, my headache and apprehension had gone away. Let the American come with all his might, we were going to be ready for him.

Macalister arrived wearing the same clothes he had worn the night before—the velvet jacket, the Hawaiian shirt—in combination with a pair of snakeskin boots. My parents made him take the boots off. He did not complain or try to get out of it, even as I unsuccessfully attempted to arrange a dispensation for him. "It is normal custom," Father said. "Bosnian custom." Sitting on a low, shaky stool, Macalister grappled with his boots, bending his ankles to the point of fracture. Finally, he exposed his blazingly white tube socks and lined up his boots against the wall, like a good soldier. Our apartment was small, socialist size, but Father pointed the way to him as though the dining room were at the far horizon and they needed to get there before the night set in.

Macalister followed the direction with a benevolent smile, possibly bemused by my father's histrionics. Our dining room was also a living room and a TV room, and Father seated Macalister in the chair at the dining table that faced the television set. He was given the seat that had always been contentious in my family, for the person sitting there could watch television while eating, but I don't think Macalister recognized the honor bestowed upon him. CNN was on, but the sound was off. Our guest sat down, still appearing bemused, and tucked his feet under the chair, curling up his toes.

"Drink?" Father said. "*Viski? Loza?*"

"No whiskey," Macalister said. "What is *loza*?"

"*Loza* is special drink," Father said. "Domestic."

"It's grappa," I explained.

"No, thanks. Water is just fine."

"Water. What water? Water is for animals," Father said.

"I'm an alcoholic," Macalister said. "I don't drink alcohol."

"One drink. For appetite," Father said, opening the bottle of *loza* and pouring it into a shot glass. He put it in front of him. "It is medicine, good for you."

"I'll take that," I said, and snatched it before Macalister's benevolence evaporated; I needed it anyway.

My mother brought in a vast platter with cut-up smoked meat and sheep cheese perfectly arrayed, toothpicks sticking out like little flagpoles without flags. Then she returned to the kitchen to fetch another couple of plates lined with pieces of spinach pie and potato pie, the crust so crisp as to look positively chitinous.

"No meat," Mother said. "Vegetation."

"Vegetarian," I corrected her.

"No meat," she said.

"Thank you," Macalister said.

"You have little meat," Father said, swallowing a slice. "Not going to kill you."

Then came a basket of fragrant bread and a deep bowl brimming with mixed vegetable salad.

"Wow," Macalister said.

"That's nowhere near the whole thing," I said. "You'll have to eat until you explode."

On the soundless TV there were pictures from Baghdad—two men were carrying a torn-up corpse with a steak tartare–like mess instead of a face, the butt grazing the pavement. American soldiers up to their gills in bulletproof gear pointed their rifles at a ramshackle door. A clean-shaven, suntanned general stated something inaudible to us. From his seat, Father glanced sideways at the screen, still munching the meat. He turned toward Macalister, pointed his hand at his chest, and asked: "Do you like Bush?" Macalister looked at me—the same fucking bemused smile stuck on his face—to determine whether this was a joke. I shook my head: alas, it was not. I had not expected Macalister's visit to turn into such a complete disaster so quickly.

"*Tata, nemoj,*" I said. "*Pusti čovjeka.*"

"I think Bush is a gaping asshole," Macalister said, un-fazed. "But I like America and I like democracy. People are entitled to their mistakes."

"Stupid American people," Father said, and put another slice of meat into his mouth.

Macalister laughed, for the first time since I'd met him. He slanted his head to the side and let out a deep, chesty growl of a laugh. In shame, I looked around the room, as though I had never seen it. The souvenirs from our African years: the fake-ebony figurines, the screechingly colorful wicker bowls, a carved elephant tusk, a malachite ashtray containing entangled paper clips and Mother's amber pendants; a lace handiwork whose delicate patterns were violated by prewar coffee stains; the carpet with an angular-horse pattern; all these familiar things that had survived the war and displacement. I had grown up in this apartment, and now all of it seemed old, coarse, and anguished.

Father went on relentlessly with his interrogation: "You win Pulitzer Prize?"

"Yes, sir," Macalister said. I admired him for putting up with it.

"You wrote good book," Father said. "You hard worked."

Macalister smiled and looked down at his hand. He was embarrassed, perfectly devoid of vainglory. He straightened his toes and then curved them even deeper inward.

"*Tata, nemoj,*" I pleaded.

"Pulitzer Prize, big prize," Father said. "Are you rich?"

Abruptly, it dawned on me what he was doing—he used

to interrogate my girlfriends this way to ascertain whether they were good for me. When they called or stopped by, not heeding my desperate warnings, he would submit them to a brutal series of questions. What school did they go to? Where did their parents work? What was their grade point average? How many times a week did they plan to see me? I tried to forbid his doing that, I warned the girlfriends, even coached them in what they should say. He wanted to make sure that I was making the right decisions, that I was going in the right direction.

"No, I'm not rich. Not at all," Macalister said. "But I manage."

"Why?"

"*Tata!*"

"Why what?"

"Why you are not rich?"

Macalister gave out another generous laugh, but before he could answer, Mother walked in carrying the final dish: a roasted leg of lamb and a crowd of potato halves drowning in fat.

"*Mama!*" I cried, "*Pa rek'o sam ti da je vegetarijanac.*"

"*Nemoj da viče. On može krompira.*"

"That's okay," Macalister said, as though he understood. "I'll just have some potatoes."

Mother grabbed his still-empty plate and put four large potatoes on it, followed by a few pieces of pie and some salad and bread, until the plate was heaping with food, all of it soaked in the fat that came with the potatoes. I was on the verge of tears; it seemed that insult upon insult was being launched at our guest; I even started regretting the previous night's affronts, at least those I could remember. But Macalister did not object, or try to stop her—he succumbed to us, to who we were.

"Thank you, ma'am," he said.

I poured another shot of *loza* for myself, then went to the kitchen to get some beer. *"Dosta si pio,"* Mother said, but I ignored her.

My father cut the meat, then sloshed the thick, juicy slices in the fat before depositing them on our respective plates. "Meat is good," he said to no one in particular. Macalister politely waited for everyone else to start eating, then began chipping away at the pile before him. The food on Father's plate was neatly organized into taste units—the meat and potatoes on one side, the mixed salad on the other, the pie at the top. He proceeded to exterminate his food, morsel by morsel, not uttering a word, not setting down his fork and knife for a moment, staring down at his plate, only to look up at the TV screen now and then. We ate in silence, as though the meal were a job to be done, thoroughly and quickly.

Macalister held his fork in his right hand, the knife unused, chewing slowly. I was mortified imagining what this—this meal, this apartment, this family—looked like to him, what he made of our small, crowded existence, of our unsophisticated dishes designed for ever hungry people, of the loss that flickered in everything we did or didn't do. With all the cheap African crap and all the faded pictures and all the random remnants of our prewar reincarnation, this home was the museum of our lives, and it was no Louvre, let me tell you. I was fretting over his judgment, expecting condescension at best, contempt at worst. I was ready to hate him. He munched his allotment slowly, restoring his benevolent half-smile after every morsel.

He liked the coffee, he loved the banana cake; he washed down each forkful with a sip from his demitasse; he actually grunted with pleasure. "I am so full I will never eat again," he said. "You're an excellent cook, ma'am. Thank you very much."

"It is good food, natural, no American food, no cheeseburger," Mother said.

"I will ask you question," Father said. "You must tell truth."

"Don't answer," I said. "You don't have to answer." Macalister must have thought I was joking, for he said: "Shoot."

"My son is writer, you are writer. You are good, you win Pulitzer."

I knew exactly what was coming.

"Tell me, is he good? Be objective," Father said, pronouncing the word "obyective."

"*Nemoj, tata,*" I begged, but he was unrelenting. Mother was looking at Macalister with expectation. I poured myself another drink.

"It takes a while to become a good writer," Macalister said. "I think he's well on his way."

"He always like to read," Mother said.

"Everything else, lazy," Father said. "But always read books."

"When he was young man, he always wrote poesy. Sometimes I find his poems, and I cry," Mother said.

"I'm sure he was talented," Macalister said. Perhaps Macalister had in fact read something I wrote. Perhaps it was that I was drunk, for I was holding back tears.

"Do you have children?" Mother asked him.

"No," Macalister said. "Actually, yes. He lives with his mother in Hawaii. I am not a good father."

"It is not easy," my father said. "Always worry."

"No," Macalister said. "I would never say it's easy."

Mother reached across the table for my hand, tugged it to her lips, and kissed it warmly.

At which point I stood up and left the room.

He had drunk water from Baščaršija, but he had no trouble forgetting Sarajevo. Not even a postcard did he ever send us; once he was gone from our lives, he was gone for good. For a while, every time we talked on the phone Father asked me if I had spoken with my friend Macalister, and I never had, whereupon Father would suggest it would be good for me to stay friends with him. Invariably, I had to explain that we had never been and never would be friends. "Americans are cold," Mother diagnosed the predicament.

I did go to see him when he came to Chicago to read at the library. I sat in a back row, far from the stage, well beyond the reach of his gaze. He wore the same Birkenstocks and white socks, but the shirt was no longer Hawaiian. It was flannel now, and there were blotches of gray in his Bakelite hair. Time does nothing but hand you down shabbier and older things.

He read from *Nothing We Say*, a passage in which Cupper flipped out in a mall, tore a public phone off the wall, and then beat a security guard well beyond unconscious with the handset, until he found himself surrounded by the police aiming guns at him:

The feral eyes beyond the cocked guns glared at Cupper. His hand was suspended midair over the security guard, the blood-washed earpiece ready to break the man's face completely open. The security guard whimpered and gurgled up a couple of pink bubbles. The cops were screaming at him, but Cupper could hear nothing—they opened and closed their mouths like dying fish. He recognized they were burning to shoot him, and it was their zeal that made him want to live. He wanted them to keep being bothered by his existence. He straightened up, dropped the earpiece, pressed his hands against the nape of his neck. The first kick rolled him off to the side. The second kick broke his ribs. The third one made him groan with pleasure. He turned them to hating his guts.

Macalister lowered his voice to make it more hoarse and smoky; he kept lowering it as the violence increased. Somebody gasped; the woman next to me leaned forward and put her bejeweled hand on her mouth in a delicate gesture of horror. I didn't, of course, wait in line so he could sign my book; I didn't have *Nothing We Say* with me. But I watched him as he looked up at his enthralled readers, pressing his book against their chests like a found child, leaning over the table so they could be closer to him. He smiled at them steadfastly, unflinchingly—nothing they said or did could unmoor him. I was convinced I had receded into worldly irrelevance for him; I had no access to the Buddhistish realms in which he operated with his cold metaphysical disinterest.

But I followed his work avidly; you could say I became dedicated. I read and reread *Nothing We Say* and all of his old books; on his website I signed up for updates on his readings and publications; I collected magazines that published his interviews. I felt I had some intimate knowledge of him, and I wanted to see how he turned what I knew into words. I was hoping to detect traces of us in his writing, as though that would confirm our evanescent presence in the world, much as the existence of subatomic phenomena is proven by the short-lived presence of hypothetical particles.

Finally, not so long ago, his latest novel, *The Noble Truths of Suffering*, came out. From the first page, I liked Tiny Walker, the typically Macalisterian main character: an ex-Marine who would have been a hero of the battle of Fallujah, had he not been dishonorably discharged for not corroborating the official story of the rape and murder of a twelve-year-old Iraqi girl and her entire family, *an unfortunate instance of miscommunication with local civilians.* Tiny returns home to Chicago (of all places!) and spends time visiting his old haunts on the North Side, trying vainly to drink himself *into stupor, out of turpitude.* He has nothing to say to the people he used to know, he breaks shot glasses against their low foreheads. *The city barked at him and he snarled back.* High out of his mind, he has a vision of a snake invasion and torches his studio and everything he owns in it, which is not much. A flashback that turns into a nightmare suggests that he was the one who slit the girl's throat. Lamia Hassan was her name. She speaks to him in unintelligibly accented English.

He wakes up on a bus to Janesville, Wisconsin. Only upon arrival does he realize that he is there to visit the family of Sergeant Briggs, a psychopath bastard whose idea it was to rape Lamia. He finds the house, knocks on the door, but there is nobody, only a TV with a kids' show on: *Soundlessly, facing the drawing of the sun on the wall, the children sang.* Tiny stumbles upon a nearby bar and drinks with the locals, who buy him booze as an expression of support to our men and women in uniform. He tells them that Sergeant Briggs, *a genuine American hero,* was one of his best buddies in Iraq. He also tells them about Declan, who was like a brother to him. Declan got shot by a sniper, and Briggs dragged him home under fire, got his knee shot off. At the bar, the booze keeps coming, for they are all proud of their boy Briggs. They want to hear more about what it was like over there, and Tiny tells them not to trust the newspapers, or the cocksuckers who say that we are losing the war. *"We are tearing new holes in the ass of the world,"* he says. *"We are breaking it open."*

Outside, snow is piling up. Tiny steals a pickup truck parked outside the joint and goes to Sergeant Briggs's house.

This time, he does not knock on the door. He goes around to the back, where he exposes himself—*hard and red, his dick throbbing*—to a little girl who is rolling up a big snowball. The girl smiles and looks at him calmly, *untroubled by his presence, as though she were floating in her own aquarium.* He zips himself up and walks back to the truck, stepping gingerly into his own footprints.

In the stolen pickup, he drives farther north, to the Upper Peninsula. Declan came from Iron Mountain. Declan is dead, it turns out, but Tiny talks to him as he drives through a snowstorm. Declan lost his mind after the *unfortunate instance.* Briggs forced him to get on top of the girl, taunted him when he could not penetrate her. Tiny watched over him afterward, because Declan was ripe for suicide. And then he deliberately walked into an ambush, shooting from the hip. Briggs dragged home a corpse.

In the midst of a blinding blizzard, a bloody wall, ten foot tall, emerges before Tiny. He brakes before he hits it. He steps out of the pickup and walks through the wall, like a ghost. He arrives in Iron Mountain in the middle of the night. He wakes up freezing in a vast parking lot. *Everywhere he looked, there was nothing but immaculate whiteness.* His clothes are soaked in blood, though he has no cuts or wounds on his body. He rubs the stains with snow, but the blood has already crusted.

He finds Declan's parents' house. Before he rings the bell, he notices that in the trunk of his pickup is a gigantic deer with intricate antlers, the side torn open. Tiny can see the animal's insides, pale and thoroughly dead. *The deer's eyes stuck wide open, as big as paperweights.*

Declan's parents know who Tiny is, Declan spoke about him. They are ancient and tired, tanned with deep grief. They want Tiny to stay for dinner. Declan's mother gives him her son's old shirt, far too big for him. She hasn't washed it since Declan left. Tiny changes in an upstairs room that smells sickeningly of apple-and-honeysuckle Air Wick. On the walls are faded photos of African landscapes: a herd of elephants strolling toward sunset; a small pirogue with a silhouette of a rower on a vast river.

But it was only when they sat down to eat that I recognized Declan's mother and father as my parents. The old man asks incessant questions about Iraq and war, keeps pouring bourbon into Tiny's glass over Mother's objections. Mother keeps bringing in the same food—meat and potatoes and, instead of spinach and potato, apple and rhubarb pies. She insists that Tiny drink water, for she can see that he is too drunk already. Father segregates his food on the plate. There is absolutely no doubt—everything bespeaks my parents, the way they talked, the way they ate, the way Declan's mother grabs Tiny's hand and kisses it, *pressing her lips into the ghost of Declan's hand.* Tiny is suddenly ravenous, and he eats and eats. He slips into telling them about the *unfortunate instance of miscommunication with local civilians,* but leaves Declan out of it. He blames himself, tells them the gory details of the rape—*Lamia's throaty moan, the flapping of her skinny arms, the blood pouring out of her*—and the old man listens to him unflinchingly, while Mother goes to the kitchen to fetch coffee. They don't seem to be troubled, as though they did not hear him at all. For an instant, he thinks that he might not be speaking, that it is all in his head, but then realizes that there is nothing inside them, *nothing except grief*. Other people's children are of no concern to them, *for there was no horror in the world outside Declan's eternal absence from it*. Mother cuts a piece of each pie, the crusts breaking, and puts the slices on a clean plate. Tiny is sobbing.

"Let me ask you a question," the old man said. "You must tell me the truth."

Tiny nodded.

"My son was a soldier. You're a soldier."

Tiny knew exactly what was coming. Let it come, he was now ready.

"Tell me, was he a good man, a good soldier?" The old man lurched forward and touched Tiny's shoulder. His hand was cold. Outside, snow was slowly falling. Each flake came down patiently, abseiling down an obscure silky rope.

"It takes a while to become a good soldier," Tiny said. "Declan was good. He was a good man."